THE LONG WAY ROUND

By the same author:

An African Season

THE LONG WAY ROUND

•

Leonard Levitt

Saturday Review Press

New York

Part One

•

Deamis remembered the Bronx. He remembered cobble-
stone streets and old ladies in black coats walking little
dogs with blankets over their backs, and the sweet-
sickening brown and black piles at curbs.

He lived in a red house with a wooden porch at 1369
Franklin Avenue. It was his grandparents' house. His
grandparents slept on the first floor. His parents slept on
the second floor. His father had a mustache. His mother
had a cough. His father wore black-and-white shoes and a
blue jacket. His mother said it wasn't a jacket, it was a
blazer.

The house had a winding staircase with a grandfather
clock at the head of the stairs. The clock chimed every
fifteen minutes. Ding dong, ding dong, it went. Dong ding,
dong ding. Every hour it chimed the number of the hour.

Deamis's room was the attic. There were pictures of
ships on the walls. Before he went to sleep his grandparents would read to him. His grandfather read to him
about trains. A boy went on a train. Negro waiters in white

3

jackets served him dinner, and porters made up berths. In the book there was a picture of a boy sleeping and the moon shining in through the window.

His grandmother read him a story about a runaway shuttle. The shuttle was one of four new subway trains in the largest city in the world, but it ran away into the tunnel and no one could find it. Its motorman found another job as a pilot on a ferry boat. Once, as the motorman waited at the subway station on his way to work, the runaway shuttle rushed past and winked at him.

His mother also read to him. His mother said if he read books he would become a rich man. "Knowledge is riches," she said. She read him stories of King Arthur who slew dragons and of Odysseus who sailed across the seas on long voyages.

One night Deamis dreamed about Odysseus. He woke up and saw Odysseus sailing on a ship through the wall. He heard Odysseus' voice. Ding dong, ding dong, it went. Dong ding, dong ding. In the dark the chimes sent shivers down his spine. Deamis screamed. He ran to his parents' room. His mother told him to sleep facing away from the wall so he wouldn't see any more ships.

At Christmas Uncle Nero came to visit. Uncle Nero had a red beard and he rubbed it against Deamis's chin. Uncle Nero played the violin. Deamis's mother said Nero wasn't his real name, his real name was Herbert.

Uncle Nero told Deamis he would teach him how to play chess. He said he had three little girls at home in St. Louis, Missouri, who were about Deamis's own age, and that he had wanted to bring them but his wife thought they were too young to travel. After Uncle Nero had gone, Deamis's mother said Nero's wife was a Catholic.

Every Friday, Deamis's mother took him to visit his

father's office on Wall Street. She said, "If your father had listened to me he could have become a rich man years ago."

First they took an elevated train that ran level with the tops of apartment houses, then sank down into the ground and became a subway. At a dimly lit station they changed for an express. Deamis held on to the edge of his mother's coat and peered into the tunnel. He watched the express as it roared toward the station like a dragon. The front of the train was the head. The lights of the train were the eyes.

Deamis liked to stand in the first car. He peered out through the front window into the tunnel and searched for the runaway shuttle. In the tunnel the express passed a local. Deamis saw the passengers inside the local. It looked as though the trains were standing still. He saw the tracks crisscrossing, and the lights blinking green and red and orange. His mother said the lights weren't orange, they were amber.

At his father's office there were desks and typewriters and adding machines and water fountains and secretaries. His father had a secretary whose name was Triscuit. She was tall—much taller than his father—and she had long blond hair. The first time she met Deamis she said, "Isn't he darling? He's so shy. And look at his red hair!" Deamis's mother said his hair wasn't red, it was copper.

When he was seven his parents moved to a new house in the country, in Atlantic Beach, Long Island, to what his mother described as a big house in a little town, which became—after her nervous breakdown and seven subsequent years of psychoanalysis—a little house in a big town. Deamis was never told the reasons for his mother's breakdown. His mother, trying to spare him, said the details were too horrible for him to know.

The new house was on the ocean and had a special ocean smell. There was a white fence around it and iron gates that swung in the wind from the sea. Now, when Deamis woke in the night, there was no grandfather clock with its chimes. Now he heard the ocean.

During the day he played on the beach. When the weather was warm, the water was blue and green and the beach was a huge white field, and he took off his shoes and ran barefoot in the sand. When the days turned cold, the sand and the water turned grey.

Deamis's first recollection of school was being called Stick or Pole or Rooster because he was a head taller and skinnier than everyone else and had red hair. He went to school in a carpool. The children in the carpool laughed at him. They said he had long white legs.

Each morning as Deamis dressed for school his mother stood behind him to make sure he put on clean underwear. "Clean underwear breeds self-respect," she said. Before he left for school she stood behind him to make sure he ate a full bowl of Cream of Wheat. "Deamis, you must eat a substantial breakfast every morning," she said.

In the carpool was a boy named FL. FL was older than the other children. He played a ukulele and sang songs in the car. Deamis learned to sing, "Folks are dumb where I come from, they ain't had any learnin'," and "There is nothin' like a dame, nothin' in the world," and "The corn is as high as an elephant's eye, it looks like it's climbing right up to the sky."

There was another boy in the carpool named Boomer. He was tiny and had large round glasses like saucers. Each morning his mother stood in the doorway and waved good-bye to him.

Boomer's house had a pebble driveway and a large lawn. Every afternoon boys played baseball on it. Every afternoon Deamis pretended he was just walking past Boomer's house and happened to see the boys playing. When they saw Deamis the boys would stop. They would call out to him, "Hey kid, you want to play?"

Once when they called "Hey kid, you want to play?", Deamis nodded. A boy, bigger than the other boys, was holding a bat. He said, "Well, it's a private game. Now get out of here before I brain you."

At home Deamis sang the songs he had learned in the carpool. His mother said, "Is that what you learned in school today?" She told him he should concentrate more on arithmetic so he would become a rich man someday. She said she would teach him how to play chess.

When he was eight Deamis went away to camp. His parents said he would love it. His mother said they would teach him to swim. She said FL went to the same camp.

His parents brought him to Grand Central Station. Deamis wore a white shirt with the name of the camp written on the front, and a green baseball cap. Scores of other little boys were also wearing white shirts with the name of the camp and green baseball caps. As they walked to the train Deamis looked back to wave good-bye to his parents, but they had already gone.

At camp they put him in a wooden cabin called a bunk. There was no toilet in the bunk so they had to go to the bathhouse. The bathhouse smelled. There were no doors on the toilets. Everyone could see.

The first night, Deamis said he wanted to go home. They sent him to the infirmary and took his temperature. The nurse gave him grapefruit juice. She asked him if he wanted to see FL. She said he could go home next day if he still wanted to.

The next day they told him he couldn't go home, but he could write his parents a letter. His mother wrote back that they would see him in four weeks on Visiting Day. Meanwhile, they made him eat Cream of Wheat for breakfast and swim in a cold, dirty lake. They said anyone who urinated in the lake couldn't go home at the end of the summer.

Once as he was walking to the lake he heard a group of boys say, "That's him." One of them said, "He thinks he's pretty tough, but he's just a tall skinny runt." They pushed him behind the bathhouse. Someone grabbed his cap. Someone punched him in the stomach and he lost his breath. Then Deamis saw FL. FL was standing far away. He waved to Deamis but Deamis was afraid to wave back. FL walked toward him. He shouted to Deamis, "Hey, didn't you . . ." Then he said, "Hey, what's going on around here?" and suddenly Deamis began to cry.

FL walked over to the boy who had taken Deamis's cap. He said, "That your hat? Well, give it back to the kid."

Suddenly FL hit the boy in the face. It made a slap, and the boy put his hands up in front of him. "Please, FL, please, FL!" he cried.

"Please, FL, please FL," mimicked FL. He said, "You chickenshit bastard. Even the kid didn't cry like that." He glared at the other boys. They were kicking imaginary stones.

FL said, "You pick on a scared skinny kid like this, but you won't even help your friend, huh?" Then he looked at Deamis. "All right," he said, "let's go."

8

As they were walking, FL said, "Anyone gives you any trouble you just call me, get it?" He said, "Most of these kids around here are so chicken you hit 'em once they'll all cry for their mothers." FL said his family was moving from Atlantic Beach to Hewlett in the fall and that he would be changing schools. "But I'll still be around to protect you if you ever need it, understand?" Deamis tried to say yes but he began crying instead, so he just nodded his head.

On Visiting Day Deamis's parents wrote that they couldn't come to camp to visit him. His mother wrote that they were visiting Uncle Nero in St. Louis and that they couldn't get back in time. She said they would be coming later in the year.

"I hope so," said Deamis's counselor.

They didn't come later in the year. They wrote they were still in St. Louis visiting Uncle Nero. His mother wrote that they swam at the country club every morning and afternoon. She wrote that Uncle Nero had three little girls Deamis's very own age, and that they were all wonderful swimmers. She wrote, "Everyone says hello."

"I didn't think they were really going to come," Deamis apologized to his counselor.

"Neither did I," said the counselor.

When Deamis came home from camp he ran through the iron gates and smelled his house's special ocean smell. Uncle Nero came for a visit, bringing his three little girls

9

who were all about Deamis's age. Every morning Uncle
Nero and the three little girls went down to the beach to
swim. They said Deamis could come too if he knew how.
Uncle Nero smiled. He said, "I hear Deamis learned to
swim in camp."

Before they went into the water the three little girls
crossed themselves. They said they were crossing themselves for protection. They said Deamis could do it too if
he wanted to. They said he didn't have to do it only when
he went swimming, he could do it all the time, like in the
morning when he woke up, or before he went to bed, or at
meals, or even at school before a test. One of the three
little girls said she herself did it whenever she went to the
bathroom.

Uncle Nero said he would teach them all to ride the
waves. He lay on his stomach, stretched his arms out in
front of him, let the waves rock him high into the crest
and sweep him down into the trough and said, "Let the
waves do all the work for you. If you're smart you'll just
lie there and enjoy it." Uncle Nero said the trick was in
catching the wave just before it broke. He said, "Sometimes the wave will be ahead of you so you'll have to
paddle hard to catch up to it. Then when you've caught it,
you take a deep breath, close your eyes, stick your head
down in it and ride it all the way to shore."

When Uncle Nero left, Deamis's parents told him he was
now a big boy. They said he was big enough to stay at
home by himself when they went out at night. His mother
said there was nothing to be afraid of because they would
leave the downstairs light on to frighten burglars away. She
said Deamis could sleep in their bed until they came home.
It was a big bed. Deamis tried to reach across from
corner to corner. When he woke in the night in the big bed

and they weren't there and he heard the ocean, Deamis imagined his parents had been killed by burglars. He would creep down the stairs and watch for them by the lights of passing cars until he fell asleep again on the living room floor.

One afternoon, as Deamis was playing on the beach he saw a shadow on the sand. It was Boomer. Deamis watched Boomer pick up a piece of driftwood and walk toward him. Then Boomer threw the driftwood at him. The driftwood struck Deamis just above the eye. Boomer started to run away. For a second, Deamis stared after him. He thought of FL and what FL had said. Then he ran after Boomer.

Boomer scampered across the sand, ducked down under a fence and dashed into the street toward his house. He ran up his pebble driveway. As he reached the steps of his house Deamis caught him. He grabbed Boomer round the legs and sat on his stomach. Boomer started to howl. The front door opened and Boomer's mother appeared. She looked at Boomer lying across the driveway and Deamis sitting on his stomach and she screamed. Sitting on Boomer's stomach, the cut over his eye bleeding down his face, Deamis started to cry. Boomer's mother brought them inside and made them peanut butter sandwiches, frankfurters sliced down the middle and hot chocolate. She washed Deamis's face with a warm washcloth and wiped the cut above his eye with a Q-tip and iodine. She made Boomer apologize to Deamis for throwing the stick at him and she made Deamis apologize to Boomer for sitting on his stomach.

After that, Deamis went to Boomer's house every day after school. Boomer's driveway was always filled with cars and there were always ladies sitting at long tables in

11

Boomer's living room playing cards. Every day there were different cars. Every day there were different ladies.

Boomer explained the ladies were playing gin rummy. He said his father played with the men at night and that his father was one of the greatest gin rummy players in the whole country. Boomer said he also knew how to play. He said his mother had taught him and that he also knew about Hollywood, schneiders, boxes, knocking, undercutting, ginning off, and holding a card out of the deck without his opponent's ever knowing. Boomer said he loved his mother better than his father because his father wanted to send him away to boarding school, but his mother wouldn't let him because she loved Boomer best in the whole world. He said once when he had gotten angry at her he had stolen an earring from her pocketbook and flushed it down the toilet and when she couldn't find it she had fired the maid. Boomer said he might teach Deamis how to play gin rummy someday when he got to know him better and felt he could trust him.

In the meantime he taught Deamis shit, cock, prick, bastard, cunt, fuck and fucking bastard. He said he had an older sister named Frannie who was probably the biggest cunt in the whole country. One day Deamis met Frannie. She said to Boomer, "Hey you little jerk-off, who's your tall skinny friend?"

Boomer said, "Fuck you, you cunt."

Boomer also taught Deamis about the New York Knickerbockers, the New York Rangers, the New York football Giants and the Brooklyn Dodgers and where Deamis could always find them on the radio late at night when his parents thought he was asleep. He taught Deamis how to read the standings. He said it was also important to know the farm teams because they had the players of tomorrow. He said the Dodgers had Triple A teams at Montreal, Canada, in the International League, St. Paul, Minnesota, in the American Association, and Hollywood, California, in the Pacific Coast League; Double A teams at Fort Worth, Texas, in the Texas League and Mobile, Alabama, in the Southern Association; and a single A team at Elmira in the Eastern League. Boomer said that Elmira and Fort Worth were just "working agreements."

Boomer said his father always bet on games and that sometimes he took him on his birthday. "I sure am lucky to have a father like that," Boomer said.

At home Deamis asked his mother why she didn't make him peanut butter sandwiches, hot chocolate, or frankfurters sliced down the middle. His mother asked, "Why can't you be as good as Boomer in arithmetic?" She said that if he didn't improve in arithmetic he wouldn't stand much chance of becoming a rich man. She said she would ask his father to teach him chess.

At dinner Deamis asked his parents whom they loved best in the whole world. They were having lamb chops. His mother said, "I love your father best and he loves me best, isn't that right, Walter?" His father took a bite of his lamb chop. He looked up at her and made a face, "Shit," he said.

Boomer also showed Deamis how to shoot holes in his garage windows with his pellet gun. He called the gun his arsenal. He showed Deamis how to light fires in the garage by taking old rags and sprinkling them with turpentine and how to make fires in the woods behind his house from wood chips and dry leaves.

"The trick is to keep them small so they'll go out by themselves," Boomer said.

Boomer said that at night he shot cats. He called it

hunting. He said, "They come around here when they think everyone's asleep. They can't come trespassing on my property. I'm king of my property."

One night Boomer invited Deamis to go hunting with him. They climbed a ladder outside the garage onto the roof. "They're all over here," said Boomer. "But some of them are black so you can't see them."

Boomer whispered, "There's one." He pointed to the bushes, near the woods. He raised the gun to his eye. It went "pop." Deamis saw the cat scamper under the bushes into the woods. Later that night Boomer shot a cat. After the pop there was a squeal. The cat was lying on the ground.

"We can't leave it there," said Boomer. "Go down and throw it into the woods."

Deamis looked at him. "Don't worry," said Boomer, "I'll keep you covered."

Deamis crept down the ladder. He was suddenly afraid of the cat. It was lying on the ground. Its head was lying on the ground. It looked like scrambled eggs. He picked it up by the tail. It felt very warm. He threw it into the woods. It made a soft thud as it brushed the bushes.

Boomer kept his arsenal in a special part of the garage he called the workshop. There were also two saws and a vise and two cages. Boomer called the cages his laboratory.

One day Boomer said he had filled up his cages. When Deamis walked back to the workshop there was a snake lying in the floor of the cage. "I got it this morning," said Boomer. "It just came in from Treflik's." He said, "I've got some food for it coming in next week. His name is Hammond." Boomer explained that snakes like Hammond ate only once every two weeks.

The next week a big box with perforated holes came.

Inside were white mice. They were squeaking. Boomer took two of the mice and put them in Hammond's cage. He put the rest in the second cage. The mice ran over Hammond, who was lying on the floor of the cage.

Boomer said, "When he's hungry he'll gobble them up." He said they should stay and watch Hammond eat them. He said they should come each afternoon and wait for Hammond to eat the mice. "Sometimes these things take time," said Boomer.

After Deamis went home, Boomer phoned him to give him a report. In the mornings he reported to him in the carpool. In the afternoons after school they sat in the garage waiting for Hammond to get hungry. Boomer said they had a good chance because he thought snakes usually ate in the afternoon.

One afternoon when they arrived in the workshop the mice were gone and Hammond had a big lump in his throat. Boomer said, "He can't do that to me. I am the king of my property." He suggested that they starve him next time. He said they wouldn't give him another mouse for a month. "That way he'll be so hungry he'll gobble it up as soon as we throw it in there."

Then Boomer said, "Now let's have some fun." He took a mouse out of the box and put it in the vise. The mouse started to squeak. Boomer tightened the vise. The mouse was still squeaking. Deamis put his hands over his ears. Boomer tightened it more until there was a soft crunch sound. The mouse stopped squeaking. Boomer opened the vise. The mouse fell to the ground.

After Hammond died three weeks later, Boomer took Deamis into the woods and showed him how to beat up Arthur Abbot.

"I never told anyone about Arthur Abbot before,"

Boomer said. "I didn't want anyone else to know about him because I want him all for myself."

Boomer showed Deamis how to lie in wait for Arthur Abbot in the woods. "While we're here," he said, "I might as well show you the difference between dry and green wood in case you ever want to start some fires by yourself."

Then he pointed to a little boy who was even smaller than Boomer himself and who wore even thicker glasses. The little boy was playing with two poodles in his back-yard. "That's him," said Boomer. He said they shouldn't go too close to the house when they planned to beat up Arthur Abbot because his mother might see. He said the only time they should go up close was when they were hungry because Arthur Abbot's mother always invited them inside for hot chocolate.

They would sit in the high grass at the edge of the woods and watch Arthur Abbot play with the poodles. Arthur Abbot sat on the ground and threw a ball into the woods for them to bring back. When he threw the ball too far, Boomer would snake along the bushes and pick it up and then pet the poodles when they came. When the dogs didn't return, Arthur Abbot would come into the woods. "Now we've got him where we want him," said Boomer.

Sometimes, though, Boomer said he would be merciful. "Hello, Arthur," he would say when he appeared, "Want to play with us?"

Other times he would play the king. He would say, "Hey kid, what are you doing in my woods?" Then Arthur Abbot's jaw would tremble and he would try to run home. Boomer would grab him. "Now see what your mother can do," he would shriek at Arthur Abbot, who put his hands in front of his face and cried, "Mercy, king! Mercy, have mercy!"

Once when Arthur Abbot ran away, he reached his backyard before Boomer tackled him. As Boomer was pulling him back into the woods Arthur Abbot's mother appeared. "Why hello boys, how nice to see you," she said. "Why don't you come inside for some hot chocolate?"

For Halloween Boomer taught Deamis how to trick-or-treat. He told Deamis to sneak as many eggs out of his refrigerator as he could. He said he was supplying the bags, so Deamis should supply the eggs.

Boomer said they would throw the eggs at anyone who didn't give them a trick-or-treat, including anyone who wasn't home. Boomer said if anyone wasn't home on Halloween it meant they didn't want to give you anything. "They're mean people who don't like kids," he said, "and they deserve whatever they get." He added, "And don't be fooled by people who give you only small things like pennies or single pieces of candy. If they don't give us a real trick-or-treat, we let 'em have it."

But all the houses gave them real trick-or-treats. They either dumped trick-or-treats into their bags, or let them take handfuls from inside their homes. Boomer said he was waiting for the one that didn't give them anything. "They're the best kind," he said.

Finally, at one house, no one answered the door. Deamis said they should ring the bell again because there was a light on inside. "No," shouted Boomer. "Now we've got 'em where we want 'em. Now we let 'em have it." He said Deamis could have the first shot because they were his eggs. Deamis looked at Boomer. "Don't worry," said Boomer, "I'll keep you covered."

He handed Deamis an egg. "Fire!" he cried.

Deamis threw the egg at the door, which was white. The egg splashed against it and dripped down toward the door-knob.

The door opened and a lady came outside. She looked around to see who was there. She had a large bag in her hand.

Suddenly another egg splattered above her head on the door. "Trick-or-treat," shouted Boomer, and ran off into the night.

Deamis stood still. For a second he wondered whether he should go up to her and help clean off her door. A car passed. The lady shouted and the car stopped. A man got out. He started toward the house. The lady shouted again. She pointed toward Deamis. The man ran toward Deamis.

Deamis ran. He ran across the lawn. He could hear the man behind him. He could hear his footsteps. Deamis ran through the bushes, through the high grass into the woods, and between low branches. He was clutching his bag, afraid to drop it. He felt the wind blowing in his face and tears in his eyes.

He ran until he was through the woods. He ran until he could hear the ocean. He ran until he found himself staring up at a house with a white fence around it and iron gates that swung in the wind from the sea. There were no lights on inside. The house was black.

The wind bit at Deamis's neck, and he tugged at his collar. He wondered where Boomer had run to. He wondered where the people in the house had gone. He thought of what Boomer had said about including people who weren't home on Halloween, about mean people who didn't like kids. He felt his hand sliding into his bag and his fingers wrapped themselves around an egg.

18

He stared again at the house. In the darkness he felt its coldness. Suddenly he realized he was staring at his own house.

Boomer also allowed Deamis to play baseball with his friends on his large lawn. Before Deamis was permitted to play, Boomer said he would have to learn the ground rules. Boomer said one of the boys played catcher for both sides and was the umpire. He was the boy who had said to Deamis, "Well, it's a private game. Now get out of here before I brain you." His name was Michael Myles.

Michael Myles said, "The ground rules are these: the newest player has to crawl under the bushes to bring back balls in foul territory. Anyone who doesn't, the umpire beats them up."

In the fall they declared the baseball season over and moved to the football lawn behind Boomer's garage. Boomer always wanted to play baseball instead of football. Everyone told him, "The baseball season's over, Boomer." But Boomer always insisted it was still baseball weather.

The football field was narrow. Michael Myles said it was narrow so that a man couldn't run around the line like a chicken but had to run through the center of the line like a man. Michael Myles always ran through the center of the line. Whenever he ran, everyone fell down. They pretended they were tackling him. They said he bit people.

Boomer said he didn't like to play football because of his eyes, so he announced the game from the sidelines.

In winter they played basketball. Everyone said Deamis was the best basketball player. They said it was because he was so tall. But Michael Myles's team always won because he kicked people under the basket when he thought no one was looking. Boomer said basketball was his favorite sport but that he would rather announce because he was too little.

On Saturdays Boomer's father would come outside to watch them play basketball. He would stand next to Boomer, who was announcing from the sidelines, and watch them play without saying a word. Boomer confided to Deamis that his father had once said Deamis had natural moves.

One Saturday, Boomer's father told all the boys to move away because he wanted to talk to Deamis. He took a piece of chalk from his pocket and marked three Xs on different spots on the court. He said to Deamis in a soft voice, "Son, I want you to practice shooting from these spots every day, even if the other boys aren't playing." He placed his hand on Deamis's shoulder. "Get used to the backboard," he said. "Get to know every spot on it." He said every court was different, and every backboard. "Never shoot at a backboard without a net," he said. He said he would buy a metal net that wouldn't tear, so Deamis could practice come rain or shine.

Boomer's father said to Deamis, "You practice enough, son, you'll start to get *the feeling.*" He said it was hard to explain what *the feeling* was, but that Deamis would know it when he got it. "It's a gift from God," Boomer's father said, "and once you've got it, son, no one will ever be able to take it away from you."

One Saturday, Boomer's father brought another man to watch them play. Michael Myles whispered to Deamis, "I

want to look good in front of Boomer's father's friend."
He said that if Deamis scored too many points he would
beat him up after the game.

As they were leaving, Deamis heard Boomer's father's
friend say, "He's a natural, all right. You put some weight
on him and give him some confidence and Hemp will have
himself a fine one in a few years."

That night Deamis was invited to dinner at Boomer's
house. After dinner Boomer's father sat at the table in the
living room playing cards with men, who sat where the
women had sat during the afternoons. Boomer's father was
dealing.

As Boomer and Deamis entered the living room he
looked up and said to Boomer in a soft voice, "Hello,
son." He also said, "Hello, son," to Deamis. As Boomer
passed behind his father he accidentally hit his father's
arm, spinning the cards to the ground like fluttering leaves.
Quick as a snake, Boomer's father spun around in his seat,
grabbed Boomer's shirt and hissed through clenched teeth,
"You myopic little bastard."

Boomer's mother screamed. She rushed into the living
room and pulled Boomer away. Afterward Boomer told
Deamis his father hated him because he was little and had
bad eyes. He said to Deamis, "He only likes *you* because
you're a natural in basketball."

When Boomer didn't want to play ball he would take
Deamis to the village for hot chocolate. "You've got to
watch out for those village kids," he said. "They're tough,
and when they curse, they really mean it!"

Boomer took Deamis to a store called The Sweet
Shoppe. The store was run by three men Boomer knew.
He called them the Guineas. "That's what my father calls
them," he said. "You like *him,* don't you?"

The Guineas stood behind the counter in white aprons. One was called Moose, another, Gus, and the third, Felix. Moose had a large, bald head. Gus had white hair and a white walrus mustache. Felix looked like anyone else. He was married to a woman named Marie. Sometimes Marie also worked behind the counter. She wore a blue apron.

When they came into the store the Guineas would gather round them and say to Boomer, "Hayadune kiddo? Hazzaoleman? Ze makany doe atta nagseze days?"

Once Boomer's father took them to the Guineas. The Guineas all gathered round him and shook hands. They pointed to Deamis and said, "He yours too?" After that the Guineas said "Hayadune kiddo," to him also.

One day, as they were walking home, two village kids stopped Boomer and pulled him into an alley. One of them was a big kid with blond hair. The other had a purple tooth.

"What do you want?" Deamis asked. The big kid turned around and pushed him. He said, "Hey Tinker, give it to the tall skinny kid."

Tinker pushed Deamis into the alley. Deamis pushed him back. Tinker pushed Deamis again. Deamis wasn't sure what to do. He wanted Boomer to help him, but he was afraid of the big kid. He tried to push Tinker out of the alley back into the street where someone could help him, but Tinker pushed him back. He braced his body for the next time Tinker pushed him, and then he sprang.

He landed across Tinker's shoulders and threw him to the ground. He heard the big kid say, "Give it to him, Tinker. Give it to the bastard."

It was hearing the word "bastard." It was hearing the village kid curse—Deamis felt the word drop down to his stomach. He felt Tinker's body wriggling beneath him. He felt Tinker gaining strength and pulling himself up. . . . He felt his own strength ebbing, Tinker suddenly breaking his hold, pushing him off, jumping to his feet and shaking himself free, and then grabbing Deamis and flinging him to the ground.

He caught a glimpse of Boomer as he fell. He was standing next to the big kid, who was pounding his fist into his hand and muttering over and over, "Kill the bastard, Tink, kill the bastard."

Tinker was on top of him. He was squeezing him. Where had his strength gone? Why were his hands limp? He looked up at Tinker and saw his purple tooth. He wondered what it meant for a person to have a purple tooth.

The big kid said, "Punch the bastard, Tink. Punch him!" And then Tinker's fist came down. It smacked across Deamis's nose, and he felt tears in his eyes. "See if you can make him cry, Tink, see if you can make the bastard cry."

Deamis didn't cry. He didn't cry when a passerby chased Tinker and the big kid away and told Deamis and Boomer to go home. He didn't cry when he and Boomer were walking past their friendly lawns and trees. He didn't cry when he came to his house, when he went through the iron gates and opened the door and smelled his house's special smell.

Only when he saw his mother standing at the head of the stairs with her hands on her hips—only when he ran up to her and tried to tell her what had happened—only then did Deamis begin to cry.

The doorbell rang. His mother went down to answer it. "Come down here, Deamis," she called.

He walked downstairs to where his mother was standing outside the door. She was talking to someone. It was the big kid. Deamis saw his blond hair and Tinker's purple tooth. He heard his mother saying, "These boys say you're afraid of them, Deamis. They say you ran away from them."

He heard his mother saying, "Go out there, Deamis, go out there and fight them! I want you to fight them, Deamis."

He was standing on the front lawn. Tinker was rolling up his sleeves. The big kid was behind him. His mother was behind him. Boomer was behind her.

Tinker came up to him and pushed him. He heard the big kid say, "All right, Tink. Kill him. Kill the bastard, Tink!"

Tinker pushed him again. Deamis put out his arm to stop him. His elbow accidentally hit Tinker's chin and he drew back in fright. He heard his mother shriek, "Hit him again, Deamis. Hit him again!" He saw her stamping her foot on the grass.

He felt a surge of power in his mother's voice. "Hit him," she shrieked. Stamp went her foot.

He swung his arm again. It was a long arm and it caught Tinker in the nose. He saw Tinker turn and look at the big kid. His mother's voice rang out, "Hit him, hit him, hit him!" Boomer's voice rang out behind hers, "Hit, hit, hit!"

He felt himself moving closer to Tinker. He saw Tinker's purple tooth. He shot his long arm out at the purple tooth.

Tinker cried out. He looked back at the big kid. Deamis's mother shrieked "Hit him, hit him, hit him." Stamp, stamp, stamp went her foot.

He felt himself closing in on Tinker. He felt Tinker moving back toward the bushes, and he felt himself following. He saw the look on Tinker's face. He saw the big kid beside him. He felt himself getting ready to spring.

He sprang. He was on top of Tinker, pushing him into the bushes. He was rolling on top of him, feeling the

24

bushes in his nose and mouth, swinging with both his arms.

His mother was yelling, "Hit, hit, hit!" Boomer was yelling, "Harder, harder, harder. . . ." The big kid was yelling. The big kid was trying to get his mother's attention.

Tinker was lying limp on the ground, gasping and crying, his mouth open and his purple tooth half sticking out. In a final gasp he suddenly pushed Deamis off him and scampered away underneath the bushes like the cat Boomer had shot at but missed.

On Boomer's birthday his father took them to a basketball game at Madison Square Garden. The Knicks were playing the Celtics. In the first game Philadelphia was playing St. Louis.

First they went to Ruby Foo's for dinner. Boomer's father knew all the waiters. They sat in the second row behind the Celtic bench. Boomer's father knew all the ushers.

In the fourth quarter with the score tied and three minutes remaining, the ball smacked Boomer in the nose and it started to bleed. Boomer started to howl. His father gave him his handkerchief and told him to sit still until the end of the game because it was very important to him. But the blood kept pouring and Boomer kept howling and people were looking, so finally Boomer's father had to take them outside and they went home.

In the car Boomer was panting as though he were out of

breath. Between pants he whispered to Deamis in the back seat that it had all been his fault from the beginning. "None of this ever happened before you started coming around—it's been bad luck for me since the first day I met you. And my father doesn't like you either. He's only nice to you because you're so good in basketball."

The next day Boomer said he wanted to start a fire in his garage. He said it would be only a little fire. It was raining and the wind was blowing. Boomer said it was a good day for a fire because the wind and the rain could blow it out.

He started the little fire in the corner of the garage. He wet the rags with turpentine and lit them.

The wind blew through the garage door. It blew the little fire. It blew the fire against the walls of the garage until the fire began to climb the walls.

Deamis wanted to run away, but Boomer said they had to stay and put out the fire. Then Boomer said they had to run away before the garage burned down. He said they should run to Arthur Abbot's house and call the fire department. He said not to worry because Arthur Abbot's mother wouldn't say anything. "She knows I'll beat up Arthur if she does," he said.

Arthur Abbot's mother wanted to know who they were calling, but Boomer said it was a private call. Deamis watched him dial a number, wondering where Boomer had learned the number, or how he knew who to ask for, or what to say. Then Boomer said they had better go home. Later Deamis heard the sound of fire engines.

The next day Boomer wasn't in school. When Deamis came to his house that afternoon, Boomer's mother said he wasn't feeling well. The next week she said Boomer had gone away to boarding school. A month later Boomer's parents moved away.

Part Two

•

Now, after school, Deamis returned to the beach. The days were growing shorter, and the water was grey. Deamis walked along the sand and thought about Boomer. He wondered if boarding school were like camp. He didn't think Boomer would like boarding school very much.

In the winter Deamis played basketball. He played on cold raw days when his fingers became stiff and numb and he had to rub them together after a basket and stick them in his pockets between shots. He played in the snow and wore galoshes. He played in the rain and dribbled through puddles. He played late into the evening, long after the others had gone, long after the street lights came on, long after the sun had gone down and the first stars had come out, and the breeze swept in from the ocean and blew the chain of the metal net, which creaked and groaned in the wind.

He felt the breeze on his face as he ran. He imagined he

was playing for the New York Knickerbockers at Madison Square Garden against the Boston Celtics and that Boomer's father was in the stands watching him play. He felt the players beside him becoming still-figures and shadows. He saw daylight between them and drove toward the basket. He was all alone and no one could catch him. And he began to get *the feeling.*

It would come to him as he sighted the basket, and felt the ball slide off his fingertips. In the air he could feel it would be good, and he would stand still and silent, watching its downward arc, waiting for the swishing clang of the metal net as the ball slid through. He wondered if this was *the feeling* Boomer's father had called a gift from God, and whether once he had it no one could ever take it away from him.

Sundays, his father—who had recently bought a maroon Chrysler Imperial convertible with whitewall tires, front and rear speakers, push-button windows, and six-way seats—would take Deamis for a drive. Sometimes the car wouldn't start. Deamis's mother would have to push it with her car.

They would drive along the water where big boats were tied to docks with ropes. Deamis's father would whistle at the boats and say, "Son, how'd you like to own one of them apples?"

"What apples?" said Deamis.

That spring Deamis found a dog. It was a black and white cocker spaniel. It followed Deamis home from school one afternoon. He named it Revolver. Deamis's mother said it wasn't a real cocker spaniel. She said it was a dirty animal that wasn't worth the food it would cost to feed him.

Deamis persuaded her to let Revolver sleep in the garage

one night. He put a blanket on the garage floor and tried to persuade Revolver to sleep on it, but when he came out to the garage the next morning Revolver was sleeping on the cement. Deamis's mother said Revolver didn't have much sense.

That afternoon, Deamis's mother had her nervous breakdown. It began when she ran over Revolver. Deamis came home from school and found the car in the middle of the lawn with Revolver bleeding under the front wheel. He knelt down and stroked his head. Revolver's eyes were still open and his back leg was twitching. "You'll be all right boy," Deamis whispered. "Your back leg is moving so you're still alive."

He was still stroking Revolver's head when the police came and led him away. His mother had locked herself in her bedroom. Deamis heard her coughing and shouting to the police that she wasn't coming out for less than $10,000, cash or certified check.

When Deamis's father came home he called up Uncle Nero in St. Louis and told Deamis his mother was going out there for a short vacation. While she was away, his father said he was bringing a woman out from the city to look after them. The woman was very tall—much taller than his father—and she had long blond hair. Deamis thought she looked just like Triscuit from his father's office. His father said her name was Crumpet.

One evening his father took them for a drive in his new Chrysler Imperial. At first he didn't think Deamis wanted to come. But Crumpet said, "Sure he does, don't you, darling?"

It was a warm night and his father put the top down. They drove along the water as Deamis and his father had on Sundays, past the boats bobbing up and down like giant houses.

Deamis's father said to Crumpet, "Do you know, I am nearly forty years old and have lived half my life?" Crumpet put her hand on the back of his father's neck. She whispered something in his father's ear. Then they both laughed.

When they returned home, his father said he would drive Crumpet back to the city. While she was packing he told Deamis not to mention anything to his mother. "You know how she is about strangers," he said.

The boy who moved into Boomer's house—which Arthur Abbot's mother claimed had been sold to pay Boomer's father's gambling debts—was named Pete. Pete was standing under the basket taking lay-ups with English on them when Deamis met him. Pete said he was from the city. He said in the city they played the best brand of basketball anywhere in the world. He said people out here in the sticks didn't play as good a brand of ball, even if they were taller.

He said, "You want to play one on one?" He said, "You pass it to me, I'll pass it back. That's how we play in the city."

Deamis passed the ball to Pete. Pete passed it back. Deamis took a jump shot. It went in. Pete said, "I guess I better play you close." He stood just in front of Deamis.

Deamis flicked his shoulder to the left, then drove past him on the right.

"Right-handed," said Pete. He threw Deamis the ball again. Deamis moved his shoulder to the right and drove past him on the left. He hit a jump shot from the corner— another from the center. Pete grabbed a rebound and Deamis batted it away. He slapped away another as Pete was dribbling. He sank the last one off his special spot on the backboard.

Afterward Pete said, "You're not a bad basketball player."

Suddenly everyone was playing basketball. Suddenly everyone wanted Deamis to be on his team.

He was asked to join a club. The name of the club was The Robbins. The Robbins wore purple jackets with two white stripes down each sleeve, the word *Robbins* written in big white script letters on the back, and their own name written in small white script on the front.

They rode English racers with three-speed gears. They traveled in packs of eight and ten. When they walked they made boys coming from the other direction step around them so they wouldn't be termed "chicken."

Sometimes the older boys came to play basketball. They also wanted Deamis to be on their team. "He doesn't say much, but he's got a helluva jump shot," they would say. The older boys had cars and rode three in the front seat. If someone sat in the back seat they said he was riding nigger.

In the eighth grade everyone crowded around Pete's desk. Pete said it showed he was very popular. Pete said he could tell if a person was popular by the way he walked down the hall. He said if a person was popular, he walked down the hall in the center of his friends. He said if he wasn't popular he walked on the outside.

Pete said there were certain things one had to do to become popular. One thing, Pete said, was to have a wave in his hair. He called it a pompadour. Pete said every morning he brushed his hair twenty-five strokes to train it to wave. Another thing, he said, was to make sure his chest was larger than his stomach. He said every morning he did fifty push-ups, twenty-five knee-bends and ten chin-ups on the bar that held his shower curtain.

Deamis began brushing his hair twenty-five times each morning. On his way to school he began looking at his reflection in store windows. He would stand sideways, hold his breath, and look over his shoulder to see whether his chest was larger than his stomach, and if his hair had a pompadour.

Pete said, "And one thing you never do is take a shit in school." He said once when he wasn't feeling well he told everyone he was going for a walk and went into the bathroom. He said, "I waited inside until no one was around so they couldn't see me when I came out. I'd never give anyone the satisfaction."

Pete also said that Deamis wasn't really that good in basketball. Deamis hated Pete and he knew Pete hated him, so they became best friends.

On Saturday nights the girls in their class had parties in their basements. The girls stood in a corner and played records by the Coasters, the Drifters, the Chiffons, and the Temptations, and giggled. The boys stood in another corner and talked about basketball. Sometimes the older boys came to the parties. They stood in their own corner.

The girls wore white socks and loafers with pennies in

them. Some girls wore sweaters. Pete said he liked the girls better who wore sweaters. He said it showed if they had anything. He said the girls here didn't have as much as the girls in the city.

Sometimes a boy dislodged himself from his corner and went to the girls' corner. He would pull out a girl, and they would stand in the center of the floor, clutching tightly together and swaying to the music without speaking. When the record was over they would return to their own corners without a word or glance.

Sometimes the older boys smoked cigarettes. Sometimes the girls smoked. Sometimes Pete smoked. He said it relaxed him.

At one party an older boy asked Deamis if he had ever done it. The older boy said, "You can do it right here. Just put your hand in your pocket. Don't worry," he said, "no one can see."

After the parties the boys all went to Marinaro's Tavern near the Long Island Railroad station for pizza. Marinaro's was where the older boys went. The older boys said Marinaro's was where Hemp and his twin brother The Sheik hung out. Hemp was the coach for Lawrence High. The Sheik was the coach for Hewlett. They were both short and thin and had large beaked noses. Hemp had a cauliflower left ear. The Sheik had a cauliflower right ear. The older boys said it was from a fight they had had when they were coaching together upstate. The older boys said they hated each other because basketball was the only thing that mattered to them. They said Hemp was jealous of The Sheik because The Sheik had won more championships and that The Sheik was jealous of Hemp because Hemp had more girl friends.

Once the boys actually saw Hemp come into Marinaro's. He sat by himself at the end of the bar and drank a glass of beer. Then he left.

The boys in Deamis's class sat in booths against the wall and tried to overhear what the older boys were saying. The older boys talked about basketball. They talked about FL. FL had been the star of Hewlett High five years before, and he had won basketball scholarships to Yale and Michigan State. They said there was no telling how good he might have become except that he had been injured in the Lawrence–Hewlett championship game in his senior year and had lost the sight of one eye. Pete said he had heard FL wasn't really that good. He said he'd heard FL just had guts.

Saturdays, some boys had Bar Mitzvah parties. Deamis's mother, who had completed her second year of psychoanalysis, said that if Deamis felt left out, he could have a Bar Mitzvah party too.

"It just so happens that you are four-thirteenths Jewish," his mother said. "Your grandfather is part Jewish and you have a Jewish aunt. And frankly, sometimes I'm not so sure about your Uncle Nero."

"Four-thirteenths?" asked Deamis.

"Now Deamis," his mother said, "you know you never were very good in arithmetic."

The Bar Mitzvahs were held at hotels and nightclubs in New York City. Deamis went to El Morocco and the Copacabana, to the Versailles Room at the Hotel St. Regis, the Quadrille Room at the St. Moritz, the Savoy Suite at the Plaza, the Crystal Ballroom at the Delmonico, and the Sapphire Room at the Pierre. They went to and from each hotel in chauffeur-driven limousines.

The boy who had the Bar Mitzvah would sit at the center

of a long table called a dais. The other boys and girls sat on each side of him. Pete said the closer you sat to the boy who had the Bar Mitzvah, the more popular you were.

During the meal there was dancing. Everyone danced. The boy who had the Bar Mitzvah had to dance the first dance. He had to pick a girl. Some boys picked their mothers.

Pete said the thing to do was to get some girl who had them and dance close to her. "Don't stand for any of that stiff-arm stuff," he said. "Try to grab a couple of good feels."

On Saturdays when they didn't play basketball or go to Bar Mitzvahs they all went to the movies. There was a fat lady at the ticket window. She said she knew they were more than twelve years old and had to pay full price for a ticket. They called her Fat Fanny. Fat Fanny said she would remember them and pay them back someday.

In the movies they sat in the balcony and ate Turkish taffy, Sugar Daddies, Jujubes and Three Musketeer bars. The balcony was where the girls sat, and the older boys. Pete said he liked to sit in the balcony because he could smoke. Pete always put his arm around the girl he was sitting next to. Deamis only put his arm around the back of a girl's chair.

In the balcony there was an usher who had a big nose with holes in it. He said he knew they weren't sixteen and couldn't sit in the balcony. They called him Old Scarface. Old Scarface also said he would remember them and pay them back someday.

A girl named Lydia Jane Levy, who—Arthur Abbot's mother claimed—had posed naked for pictures on the toilet seat when she was nine, now took boys' hands and led them along the curves of her body. Lydia Jane Levy sat with her coat in her lap. "Don't worry," she said to each of them. "Nobody can see."

After a boy sat with Lydia Jane Levy he reported back to the other boys who were awaiting their turn. At first, in the seventh grade, they said, "What did you get? Did you get tit?" Later, in the eighth grade, they said, "Did you get bare tit?" Still later, in the ninth grade, they asked, "Did you get cunt?"

Pete said he wouldn't do anything with a girl in the movies if he really loved her. He said, "I'd wait until I got her back at her house." He said it was much more mature to visit a girl at her home. He said he sometimes visited three or four girls in one night. He said he only visited Lydia Jane Levy when her parents weren't home. "The only trouble with Lydia Jane Levy," he said, "is that she has a little brother who never leaves you alone."

Pete said Lydia Jane Levy called her little brother the Vonce. He said Lydia Jane Levy said it meant bedbug. Pete said he wouldn't give out the names of any other girls he visited because it might give people the wrong idea.

After one Bar Mitzvah party Lydia Jane Levy sat next to Deamis in the back seat of the limousine. There was another boy and girl sitting next to them. The girl was sitting on the boy's lap. Lydia Jane Levy said to Deamis, "Do you want me to sit on yours?"

She slid onto his lap and put her arm on his shoulder. She whispered, "I like it better standing up. That way you can feel all parts of the body." Suddenly she was kissing him. Deamis felt her mouth opening. He could feel her tongue against his lips, pushing them open, sliding over his teeth and pressing, soft and wet and warm like a Sugar Daddy or Turkish taffy.

Lydia Jane Levy slid his hand under her coat. She slid

her hand under his coat. He heard her whisper, "You touch mine and I'll touch yours."

She touched him. He felt his body jump. "Don't worry," she murmured, "no one can see."

She rubbed her hand against him. Back and forth it went, back and forth. Deamis tried to look over at the couple next to him. He didn't want them to see . . . he wanted them to see so they could stop her. . . . But she didn't stop. Then he didn't want her to. It was tickling. It was tickling, and he was squirming in his seat. It was tickling and his whole body was tingling, while the limousine purred through the night, no one seeing, no one speaking, as though they were all party to this frightening, delicious, maddening feeling. And then Deamis felt he was about to burst. He felt himself growing warmer and warmer. He wanted to shout, but he was afraid. He wanted to laugh, but he was ashamed.

The cab lurched to a halt. The driver swung around and stared at them. In one final stroke Lydia Jane Levy flung her hand from him, jumped off his lap, slammed the car door and ran up her path to her house, leaving him alone in the back seat with the other couple, shaking, quivering, and unable to wait until he reached home to see what she had done to him.

ııı

One night Pete took Deamis when he went visiting. Her name was Susan Stickwell. Susan Stickwell was known to be very popular and very mature. "Why, hello, Pete," she said when she opened the door, "how nice of you to stop by."

Susan Stickwell's father was lying on the couch. He was wearing Bermuda shorts and red tennis sneakers, he was reading a book by S. J. Perelman and he was chuckling. Two white kittens were playing under the couch. Every time Susan Stickwell's father chuckled, the white kittens sat up and looked at him.

Susan Stickwell said, "I'm very glad to see you both." She bent down and said to the two kittens under the couch, "Edgar and Evelyn are glad to see you too, aren't you Edgar and Evelyn?" Susan Stickwell said they also had a dog named Saunders, currently at the vet's being spayed, a turtle named Paris, and two goldfish named Clement and Roscoe.

Susan Stickwell and Pete began talking about school. They talked about other girls in the class. Susan Stickwell's father got up from the couch and went into the bedroom. Susan Stickwell's mother came into the room and turned on the television. Susan Stickwell asked if they cared for anything to eat. She got up and brought in a bowl of fruit. Pete ate an apple. Deamis said he wasn't hungry. Then Susan Stickwell's father came back into the room and said wasn't it about time they both went home? Susan Stickwell said, "Thank you both for coming." She said she was very glad to have seen them.

On the way home Pete said he hadn't tried anything with her because her parents were in the room all the time. "I also didn't think I should because you were there," he said. "It might not be good for her reputation."

The next week one of Susan Stickwell's girl friends told one of Deamis's friends that Susan Stickwell had a crush on him. Susan Stickwell's girl friend said she thought it was because of his red hair. She said Deamis should call Susan Stickwell and ask her out. Deamis knew Susan Stickwell was very popular so he was afraid not to.

Deamis had never asked a girl out before. He wasn't sure what to say on the phone. He said he thought they might go to the movies on Saturday. Susan Stickwell said she would love to go to the movies. She said Saturday night was a much more mature time.

Deamis had never been to the movies with a girl at night. He knew older boys went. He was afraid of Fat Fanny at the ticket window and Old Scarface in the balcony. He hoped Susan Stickwell's father wasn't there when he picked her up.

But Susan Stickwell answered the door herself. While they were walking to the movies she talked about the girls in their class, those she liked and those she didn't, those who were real friends and those who weren't, those who were infantile and those who were mature, while Deamis thought about what he would do if, in front of Susan Stickwell, Fat Fanny or Old Scarface told him he couldn't pass for sixteen, or if he had to go to the bathroom.

But there was no Fat Fanny at the ticket window, no Old Scarface in the Balcony. They stepped inside to the darkness, Susan Stickwell took his arm and he slid into his seat.

Deamis was so pleased with himself that during the movie he lifted his arm not merely around the back of Susan Stickwell's chair but onto her shoulder. After the movie he was so pleased she had let his arm stay on her shoulder that he suggested they go for something to eat. Susan Stickwell said a lot of mature people went to Jahn's for ice cream.

At Jahn's there were girls Deamis had seen but never

dared speak to, and when they sat down he realized just how popular Susan Stickwell really was. An older girl came over to their table. She said, "Oh Susan, how are you?"

Deamis ordered a chocolate sundae. Susan Stickwell ordered a chicken salad on rye toast. Deamis thought that was very mature.

As they left he overheard two girls who had looked over at him and Susan Stickwell while they were eating. They were talking about them.

At Susan Stickwell's door Deamis considered kissing her good night. He wondered if she wanted him to, because she kept smiling and laughing up at him. But he didn't know what to do if she refused so he decided not to risk it.

Susan Stickwell became Deamis's girl friend. Everyone at school said they were an ideal couple. Sometimes Deamis even spoke to her. In the afternoons he walked her home from school. Susan Stickwell had an older brother named Mark, who played junior varsity basketball. In the afternoons he played in his driveway with his friends, running and shouting up and down the driveway, "Pick, pick," or, "Shot, shot."

Every afternoon Deamis watched them. He longed for the day they might need an extra man, and he would have a chance to run up and down the driveway with them in front of Susan Stickwell, shouting "Pick, pick," or "Shot, shot."

Once as he stood watching them play, Susan Stickwell came outside and stood next to him. It was growing dark and the first stars had come out. Susan Stickwell looked up at the sky. "That's our star, Deamis," she whispered. "It's so close, you can just reach up and touch it." She said, "Would you reach up and catch me a star if I asked you to, Deamis?"

She touched his arm. "Some day we'll get married, Deamis, and you'll be a vice-president, and our children will go to Ethel Walker, and we'll have a house in Connecticut with a two- and one-half-acre lawn, a goldfish pond, dogs and cats, maybe even a hamster."

Susan Stickwell's mother asked Deamis if he had given any thought to where he would go in the future. She said that Mark was going to Harvard. She said, "Lester and I both feel that breeding is every bit as important as riches."

One Saturday afternoon, Deamis and Susan Stickwell went to Rockaway Playland Amusement Park. They went with Pete and Lydia Jane Levy. Susan Stickwell asked Deamis if he knew the kind of girl Lydia Jane Levy was. She whispered to Deamis she had heard Lydia Jane Levy was extremely fast. She explained that she herself wasn't that kind of girl. "I just want to be sure you know the kind of girl I really am, Deamis."

Susan Stickwell said she wanted to go on the ferris wheel. She said it was customary for people in love to go on the ferris wheel together. A man slapped a bar across their legs. It pressed tight against him.

Pete and Lydia Jane Levy were in the car ahead of them. It was dangling in the air. Deamis saw Pete lean over and put his arm around Lydia Jane Levy. They were kissing.

Deamis decided he would finally kiss Susan Stickwell. He leaned over and put his arm around her, but when he leaned to kiss her she turned her cheek. "I never kiss in broad daylight," she said.

The ferris wheel started. They were going up in the air. Susan Stickwell was looking down below. Suddenly there was a drop. Deamis felt his stomach drop. It dropped to the bottom of the cage. He pressed forward against the bar.

The ferris wheel was going up again. Deamis took a deep breath. He pressed harder against the bar. His stomach was rolling on the floor of the car.

When they got out, Deamis tried to run to the men's room. He started running, but in the middle of the amusement park with all the people around him, with Susan Stickwell next to him, he bent over and threw up.

The next week Pete told him he had heard Susan Stickwell thought he was quite immature. Pete said he wouldn't have told him except that they were best friends.

The next month Pete announced he had a girl he was doing everything with. He said they had done it in the new houses that were being built in what used to be left field in Boomer's backyard. He said that they wrote love letters to each other, that she took taxis to his house at 2:00 A.M. after his parents had gone to sleep, that on New Year's Eve they had gone to the city and stayed at the Waldorf Astoria and that they had even heard the chambermaids whispering about them next morning.

When no one believed him, he claimed he had proof. The next day he passed out five pictures he claimed to have taken and developed himself. Although her face was obscured, the pictures strongly resembled Lydia Jane Levy. In the first picture she was in a slip. In the second she was wearing a bra and panties. In the last picture she was lying nude on the floor of one of the new houses, her legs apart, smoking a cigarette. Arthur Abbot suggested he be called Polaroid Pete.

Later in the year Deamis saw Susan Stickwell at a party. She was with an older boy, and they were smoking. Later he saw them dancing. The record was playing "Tonight You're Mine." Susan Stickwell's eyes were closed, and both her arms were around the older boy's shoulders.

Deamis took a deep breath to keep his stomach from dropping as it had on the ferris wheel. He barely had time to run outside for fear of throwing up again.

In his sophomore year Deamis was spotted by Hemp, who observed his long legs, his jump shot, discovered he had three more succulent years of eligibility and was heard to have muttered, "But he's gentle as a lamb for chrissakes." Consequently, Hemp announced he would take the boy under his wing and teach him "basics," and ordered his assistant, Getz—a crew-cut young man reputed to have earned a letter at Villanova before he was expelled for having been found in the back seat of his car with a fourteen-year-old junior high school cheerleader—to instruct Deamis in the fine arts of tripping, shoving, gouging, pushing off and landing on ankles, while Hemp himself ran alongside, screeching from the sidelines in his high-pitched whine, "Arms up like branches, elbows out like swords, you mother-humper."

In the first game of the season Deamis scored fifteen points and bruised someone's toe. In the second he scored twenty and sprained someone's finger. In the third he scored twenty-five and fractured someone's wrist. Both Hemp and Getz agreed he was showing tremendous improvement.

At the end of the year Hemp declared Deamis had

improved so much that he announced he would bring him to his summer camp in the Berkshires. "First though," Hemp said, "I got to check it out with your folks." That Sunday he visited Deamis's parents, explaining that he felt it incumbent upon him to expose the boy to the best sportsmanship and the great outdoors, two aspects of American life he thought too many youths were lacking nowadays.

"Look at it this way," he said to Deamis's mother. "We both want what's best for your boy, don't we? Well, if I develop him right he could be worth a quarter of a million to you." Hemp took Deamis's father aside and whispered, "I think I understand where *your* interests lie. Well, ballplayers like him get a helluvalot of it."

At camp, Hemp declared Deamis a counselor. "Anyone asks, you tell 'em you're a freshman at Wabash State. In Indiana. Don't worry. No one ever heard of it."

There were six little boys in his bunk. One boy had had polio. His left leg was very short and very thin and very white and he dragged it behind him like a tail. He came to the station with an envelope tied round his neck with a piece of string. On the envelope was written, *"To whom it may concern."*

Inside was a letter: "This is to introduce Kenneth. He wets his bed at night. Please be certain to take him to the bathroom before he goes to sleep. There are extra sheets in his duffel bag—just in case."

On the train another counselor said to Deamis, "That kid's parents are good for fifty dollars." He said they always paid by check at the end of the summer because they never came up to camp.

In the mornings Deamis watched the little boys in his

bunk eat Cream of Wheat for breakfast. In the afternoons he watched them swim in a cold dirty lake. At the end of the lake was a ten-foot diving board. The swimming counselor, who had white hair and wore a baseball cap and was called Pop, said each boy had to jump off the diving board or he wouldn't be able to go home at the end of the summer.

Evenings, Deamis played basketball. He played with six other counselors and five waiters who were Negroes and went to college in Alabama, and who slapped each other's palms whenever they scored a basket. They played in the dining room, which had two baskets at either end, moved the tables and chairs to the sides, turned on the juke-box (which had written on it "Oldies but Goodies"), and played to The Platters and "My Prayer," Elvis Presley and "Don't Be Cruel," Little Anthony and the Imperials and "Tears on My Pillow" and the Five Satins and "In the Still of the Night."

After the counselors scored a basket, Hemp would run along the sidelines screeching out to them as they ran downcourt, "Arms up like branches, elbows out like swords, you mother-humpers." One of the Negroes was named Stitch. He was taller than Deamis and he taught him how to block shots. Stitch said, "You got to get it before it starts to make the arc, man."

On Visiting Day Kenneth told Deamis his parents weren't coming because they were traveling. He said they would come later in the summer. Later in the summer Kenneth showed Deamis a letter. It said, "Dear Ken: We are having such a wonderful time. We swim at the country club every morning and Uncle Danny lunches with us with his two boys who are just your age, and he brings his dogs which you like so much. In the afternoon we go into town and shop and at night we go to parties, usually with the Swetsons or the Barlows. Do you remember the little Barlow boy, Jeremy? He is a year younger than you and is here with them and is such a bright, well-mannered child. Unfortunately, Ken, we will not be able to get up to camp this summer because we are staying through the end of August. We will meet you at the station. Then we will buy you lots of new toys and clothes for school. All our love, Mommy and Daddy."

"I didn't think they were really going to come," said Kenneth.

"Neither did I," Deamis wanted to say. Instead he told Kenneth he didn't have to eat Cream of Wheat for breakfast or go swimming again for the rest of the summer.

Twice a week the camp team played basketball against other camps. Before the first game they nominated a captain. Deamis nominated Stitch. But Hemp said he wanted a white. Deamis looked at Stitch. Stitch said, "Just be cool, man."

When they played at home the Negroes played with the team, but when they played away only the counselors played. Hemp said the Negroes weren't allowed to go to other camps. He said it would give the camp a bad name.

When they played away they played outdoors on cement with arc lights high around the sides of the court. The campers sat on the edges, cross-legged or on wooden benches. Some camps were co-ed and had cheerleaders who kicked their feet, and flashed their colored underwear. Deamis felt the cool summer breeze on his face as he ran. He felt the players beside him becoming still-figures and shadows. High in the lights he sighted the basket. He felt the ball slide off his fingertips, and in the air could feel it would be good, and he would stand, still and silent, watching the ball's downward arc, waiting for the swish of the net as the ball slid through.

At home games the campers filled the dining hall, stomped their feet and screamed out, "De-e-eemis." The team ran out onto the floor in a line, the first man, Stitch, bouncing the ball as he ran, the jukebox playing "Sweet Georgia Brown." Then the cheer would go up, making Deamis look down at his feet and force his jaw shut to keep himself from breaking into a grin as he raced toward the basket for his lay-up, caught the ball in mid-air, leaped toward the basket and felt he was leaping higher with each jump than he ever had before.

He came to know the thud of the ball on shiny, shellacked floors. He came to know the shouts of players, the grunts from their sweaty bodies, the wet slap of his teammates' hands on his back after he scored a basket. He came to know the crowds, to know Hemp's voice that rasped out into the night, "Arms up like branches, elbows out like swords, you mother-humpers. . . ." Until he knew every spot on the dining room floor, every spot on the Lawrence High backboard; until he could set up behind any screen, move off any pick, shove with either shoulder, knee with either knee, push off high or low, come down on anv ankle. Until he could feel an opponent coming up behind him without even turning his head, sense which way his man would break; until the roar of the crowd was but a whisper, and he could sight the basket and know in the air it was going to be good.

Until, in his senior year, he stood six foot five and they were comparing him to FL, saying he was every bit as good and then some; and the scouts from the Eastern colleges were patting his shoulder, slapping his back and taking him and Hemp to dinner; until everyone was speaking of Hemp's brilliant strategies and Deamis's natural moves and marveling at their father-son relationship; and *Newsday* predicted Lawrence was going to win the first county championship under Hemp since . . .

Except that they lost the final game to Hewlett, which had already lost once, and then Hewlett beat them in the play-off for the championship the following week. Deamis didn't play in the championship game. It happened like this:

He came down with a rebound in the first quarter of the first Hewlett game after having scored the last eight points. Someone landed on his ankle, someone else caught him with an elbow in the nose, and he went down.

Hemp leaped off the bench onto the court, shook his fist at The Sheik, who was kneeling in the middle of his players, and had to be restrained by the referee as he lunged toward him. He made Deamis lie down on the foul line and hopped around him squawking into each ear, "Son, son, speak to me, son."

When Hemp recovered he pleaded with the referee to grant him a ten-minute time-out. "Time-out?" grumbled

50

the ref. "The boy doesn't need a time-out. He needs a doctor."

They led Deamis hobbling to the bench, Hemp sobbing behind him into a large checkered handkerchief, turning every few steps to shake his fist at The Sheik, and moaning, "He'll never recover in time, he'll never recover."

Three minutes later when Hewlett had tied the score, Hemp decided Deamis had sufficiently recovered and pushed him out onto the floor. The referee walked over to Hemp and The Sheik and whispered something nobody could hear except Arthur Abbot's mother—who attended all the Lawrence home games and sat just behind the team bench and who was frequently seen in the parking lots after the games, and who claimed, the following fall—after Hemp had been discovered in his car with a twelve-year-old runaway—that the referee had warned both of them that in the light of their reputations he was prepared to initiate criminal charges, should the situation warrant it.

Hewlett called time out. When Deamis took his first shot someone landed on his ankle. Someone else caught him with an elbow in his Adam's apple. Blood spurted and Deamis twisted his head in pain. Another elbow jabbed him just above the eye. He was on the floor when they blew the whistle. They had to carry him downstairs to the locker room.

At half time a doctor examined him and announced to him and a choking Hemp that he was out for the rest of the season, but that it was nothing time wouldn't heal in a month or two. The doctor also said Deamis had sustained a nasty bruise just above his left eye. Staring at Hemp he said, "Had it been half an inch lower the boy would have been in serious trouble."

Deamis was alone in the locker room for the second half. It was eerie in its emptiness. He could hear the faraway shouts from the gym. They roared in like claps of thunder. Each time it came, he started, and strained to listen.

He peeled off his uniform and limped up the stairs to the shower. His ankle had already begun to swell. He turned on the hot water and felt it wipe across his face like a soft brush. Then he heard a final roar and then the clump of feet and voices. He was glad he was in the shower so no one could see he was crying.

As he was dressing, The Sheik came into the locker room to see him. Deamis thought it was kind of him. He told The Sheik the doctor had said it was nothing time wouldn't heal in a month or two but that he was out for the rest of the season.

"Glad to hear it," said The Sheik, breaking into a grin. He said he meant he was glad to hear Deamis would be better soon.

Deamis was the last person to leave the locker room. As he hobbled past the door he noticed Hemp sitting alone in front of his locker. His hands covered his face and his body shook with sobs. Deamis started to go over to him, to say something, to put his hand on his shoulder. Then he saw The Sheik walk over to Hemp. The Sheik was laughing.

"You tried to fool big brother, didn't you," Deamis heard The Sheik saying. "I gave you the warning when they knocked him down the first time, but you didn't get the message. You were willing to risk his eye. My boy said he would have had it if he hadn't twisted his head at the last second."

Hemp gave another sob. The Sheik gave a short laugh. "Like you got FL's," he said.

Hemp stopped sobbing and sat up. The Sheik laughed

again. Then he turned and walked to the door. In the doorway The Sheik stopped. "See you tonight at Marinaro's, you mother-humper," he shouted.

For a second, Hemp didn't say anything. Then he also laughed. "See you tonight at Marinaro's, you mother-humper," he shouted back.

At the athletic banquet, held in the gymnasium at the end of the season, Hemp spoke on the meaning of sportsmanship and fair play. He said he and Deamis had met through basketball and had developed an everlasting friendship and respect for one another through the game. He said he had brought Deamis to his summer camp where Deamis had developed a sense of responsibility and shown a love of little children equaled by few, and that he himself had treated Deamis like his own son. He added that he was justifiably proud that Deamis had recently been accepted by prestigious Dooton College, that he knew Deamis would be a credit to basketball and to the high ideals he had always tried to instill in young men through the years.

Deamis was also supposed to give a speech. Instead he simply stood up and said, "Thank you." Afterward he explained to Hemp that his ankle was bothering him and he hadn't wanted to aggravate it. But he was thinking of FL. He wondered what it felt like to be without an eye.

During the basketball season, Deamis began seeing Susan Stickwell again. She said everyone was talking about him. A few months later, Pete, who had taken Susan Stickwell out two years before and maintained she was dating Deamis on the rebound, claimed to have heard her say that Deamis was better at stuffing the ball through the net than he was between the sheets.

The Stickwells had moved away the year before. When they returned they lived in a house near the golf course. Arthur Abbot's mother said they had moved out of embarrassment when Mark was not accepted at Harvard.

Susan Stickwell told Deamis her new house was near a good place to park. She told him to turn off the headlights and turn the ignition on battery so they could play the radio. While they listened, Susan Stickwell crossed her legs, smoked cigarettes, pushed her body against his, dug her nails into his back, stuck her tongue into his ear, leaned back across the front seat, pulled him down on top of her and groaned from the back of her throat, "No, Deamis, no, no."

Driving home they played the radio and held hands. While Deamis hummed, Susan Stickwell sang the words of songs in a high squeaky voice.

Susan Stickwell told Deamis she would prefer to see him Fridays than Saturdays because Saturdays she went to New York to see her friend Little Ellie. Susan Stickwell said Little Ellie's father had a seat on the American Stock Exchange. "Mummy thinks she may be a valuable person for me to know in later life."

One Saturday night when Deamis happened to be in New York, Susan Stickwell suggested they meet and ride home together on the midnight train. Susan Stickwell said she had a date with a friend of Little Ellie's who was a sophomore at Yale. "We're going to Orsini's for dinner. It's a well-known Italian restaurant. Of course, he'll want to take me home," she said, "because he knows the kind of girl I am, but I'll only let him go as far as Pennsylvania Station." Susan Stickwell said she'd be waiting for Deamis in the third car from the front.

Deamis met her in the third car. She was sitting with her legs crossed and a *Mademoiselle* magazine in her lap, and she was smoking a cigarette. A boy was standing outside her window. He had pimples. When Deamis sat down next to her, Susan Stickwell took his arm. Through the window he saw the boy gulp.

On the train Susan Stickwell read her *Mademoiselle*. When Deamis got out at Jamaica Station he stood outside her window and waved to her. Susan Stickwell put down her magazine, looked up at him, and smiled.

After Deamis's acceptance by Dooton, he was invited to dinner at Susan Stickwell's home. First, though, Susan Stickwell made Deamis promise he would say "yes" before she told him what. She handed him a book. "Mummy wants you to read it. She says you lack breeding."

The book was *Etiquette* by Emily Post. Susan Stickwell said that if he really cared about her feelings he would read it before he came for dinner.

"Don't do it," said Pete. "It's all a trick by her mother. She's the reason we broke up. She just wants you to come for dinner so she can give you her etiquette test." He said, "She gives you things like spare ribs or duck with sauce, that you have to eat with your hands, and things like watermelon or grapes for dessert.

". . . and she watches everything. She told me I failed because I didn't point the soup spoon away from me and because I didn't put my knife and fork parallel on the far end of the plate with the knife edge pointing out." He said, "I'm telling you Deamis, you'll never pass it. But try and remember about the soup spoon."

Three days after Deamis had dinner at Susan Stickwell's house he received a postcard with the letter C+ on it. In smaller writing in red pen at the bottom were the words: "Good handling of the soup spoon, but I suggest you reread the chapter on use of the knife and fork."

Susan Stickwell became the first girl Deamis made love to although he had claimed to have had intercourse with a Negro from Far Rockaway under the boardwalk near Rockaway Playland the summer following Polaroid Pete's exposures.

It was the week before he went off to college. Susan Stickwell said she wanted to walk in the sand under the moonlight. "I've been waiting for this night a long time," she whispered. They walked along the water's edge where the sand was damp. There was no moon—only one star. "It's our star, Deamis," she said. She touched his arm. "Do you remember that day, Deamis, when I asked you to catch me a star? It seems so long ago, doesn't it?"

Suddenly Susan Stickwell stopped talking, and turned toward him. She pushed her body against his, dug her nails into his back, stuck her tongue into his ear, leaned back and pulled him down on top of her onto the sand, and groaned from the back of her throat, "Yes, Deamis, yes, yes."

He felt her wiggling beneath him. He felt the wind on his back as she lifted his shirt. He felt the sand blowing up his leg as she pulled down his trousers. And as she reached for him he thought he heard her whisper, "Take me, Deamis, take all of me." And then he felt her, warm and cool and moist and dry and smooth and soft. He lay on her with his arms outstretched as though he were riding a wave. He could feel the wave beneath him sweeping him higher and higher up on the crest, deeper and deeper down into the trough. The wave was ahead of him. He was paddling faster to catch it. Until he finally caught up to it, took a deep breath, closed his eyes, stuck his head down and rode it all the way to shore.

The next time, Susan Stickwell said they should try different positions. She said her favorite position was sitting on his lap. She said she liked it better than any other position because they could do it in broad daylight even when her parents were in the next room. In one motion she flicked off her panties and stuffed them under a cushion on the couch. Then she got up on his lap, unzipped his fly, eased herself down on him, covered them with her skirt and squeaked like a pig. "Now," she said, "no one can see."

When her parents weren't home she also removed her brassiere and bounced up and down as though she were riding a horse. Her head cocked to the side, her mouth half open, her breasts bobbed up and down, and she cupped Deamis's hands around them as though they were the reins.

Susan Stickwell said that if Deamis wanted, she would promise to teach him everything she had ever learned. She taught him how to do it on his side and on his back and from behind and kneeling and on one knee, and with one leg sticking up in the air as though he were riding a bicycle. She taught him how to bite her arms and kiss her calves and suck her toes and fingers and nipples and run his lips along her neck and down her spine and between her shoulder blades and up her thighs and over her stomach, and everywhere.

Susan Stickwell said she had two ways to come, an inside

come and an outside come. She said an inside come was when she came all the way up to her stomach and an outside come was when she came all the way down to her toes. She said that when she put the two comes together it was a combined high-voltage, A+ come.

Susan Stickwell said that if his or her parents were ever away for the weekend Deamis could sleep over or vice versa. She said after they did it they would open the bedroom window and lie naked and feel the breeze. Susan Stickwell said she liked to lie naked and feel the wind on her body more than anything else except a man.

Susan Stickwell said they could also shower together the next morning. She said, "I'll wash yours, Deamis and you'll wash mine." Susan Stickwell said she would also watch him shave. She said, "I hope you don't use an electric razor, Deamis."

Susan Stickwell said Deamis should try to get to her house before five o'clock. "That way we can do it from from five to seven." Susan Stickwell said that from five to seven was her favorite time. She said it was better than from four to six or from six to eight because from four to six she was still thinking about that day and from six to eight she would probably be so tired afterward she might fall right to sleep and not wake up until the next morning. "Then we wouldn't be able to do it again before we went to sleep," Susan Stickwell said. Susan Stickwell said the only thing worse than not doing it before they went to sleep was doing it early in the morning. "It just makes me groggy as hell all day," she said.

Susan Stickwell told Deamis she was a very sincere and honest person who knew exactly what her mistakes in life had been. She said she didn't know if Deamis knew it but that when she was younger she was always the smartest one in her class. "I was smarter than all the boys," Susan Stickwell said. "I was the fastest reader in the first grade."

Susan Stickwell told Deamis she thought it only fair to tell him that he was not the first person in her life. "Let's see," she said, "there was Mel and Dave and Dave's cousin Mark and Mark's friend Edwin and Mel, Oh! I said him already, and Timmy. Timmy was the best." Susan Stickwell said, "Tell me the truth, Deamis, do you think I'm too honest?"

Susan Stickwell told Deamis about Timmy. "We were very close," she said. "We used to go to the bathroom in front of each other and everything."

Susan Stickwell said, "Now, Deamis, I don't want you to get the wrong idea about me, but, well, I had his baby." She said, "They sent me away to Marillac Hall. In Michigan. It's Catholic, but it's very clean."

She said, "Nobody ever knew why we moved away. Mummy said it just wouldn't look right if we had stayed." Susan Stickwell said, "It cost two thousand dollars. You had to promise you wouldn't keep your baby. I had to promise I would never see Timmy again. Mummy said it was such a shame because his father is one of the largest stockholders in Olin Mathieson."

Susan Stickwell explained that there were thirty girls there. She said, "At first I just used to stay in my room and cry. I just never wanted to come out. Little Ellie was always trying to get me to come out and talk to the other girls but I never would."

Susan Stickwell said, "All the other girls there wanted their babies, so I said I did too. But really, I didn't. I mean if I had a baby I couldn't go out on dates or anything."

Susan Stickwell said, "Do you think that was dishonest of me, Deamis?"

Susan Stickwell said that Little Ellie still kept her baby's diaper in her drawer between her sweaters. "She says she'll give the diaper away when the baby's smell goes away. You know the smell I mean, Deamis, when they take it out of you and it's all wet and sticky and then they clean it and put baby powder on it and it smells so clean?"

Susan Stickwell said, "Now every time I go to Little Ellie's, she makes me look in her drawer and smell the diaper. She always asks me if I can still smell the baby smell and I always say, 'Yes,' but frankly, Deamis, I can't smell a damn thing."

When Deamis went off to Dooton, Susan Stickwell went off to a junior college outside Philadelphia. Susan Stickwell's mother told Deamis how glad she was he was going to Dooton because it was the right kind of college. She said she wanted to be sure Susan knew the right kind of people. "Quite frankly, Deamis," she said, "before we found out you were going to Dooton we weren't sure you were the right kind of person."

Susan Stickwell's mother said, "I'm only sorry they don't have sororities. I was so hoping Susan would become a Pi Phi." She sighed. "We were always better than the Kappas. Not that the Kappas weren't pretty. They were just so scatterbrained." Susan Stickwell's mother smiled. "We used to call them something that isn't very ladylike or I'd tell you, Deamis. It rhymes with Kappa so you might have some idea."

The day before Deamis was to leave for Dooton his mother announced she had some tragic news for him. "I'm sure you've been aware of certain difficulties in the past between your father and myself," she said. "I would have spoken to you of them earlier, but I wasn't certain you were old enough to understand." She said that only after the most agonizing scrutiny had she most reluctantly concluded that the only solution that would best serve the interests of all concerned was a trial separation.

Deamis's mother explained that with the settlement she was prepared to receive she was thinking of investing in Westinghouse Electric, Standard Oil of New Jersey, IBM and American Tel and Tel. "Frankly speaking," said his mother, "I'm acting solely out of concern for you in the long run. I want to be sure you get the most out of the inflationary trend in the economy."

His mother added that she was also considering the idea of going abroad as soon as she could settle most of her affairs. "I've been having some strange dreams about them lately that I haven't quite been able to resolve," she said. She added, "What strange dreams have you been having lately, Deamis?" She said that while she was away, Deamis should feel free to consult her psychiatrist any time he wished.

That night his father called to ask him if he would like to double date. "Bring your best girl," his father said. "I'll pick you kids up." Deamis said he had only one girl.

"Wait till you see her," his father said. "You'll cream in your pants."

His father picked them up in his new lavender Crown Imperial convertible that had an electric sun roof, stereo tape deck and record player in the glove compartment, warning sentinel lights with an automatic pilot, tilt and telescope steering wheel that went from parallel to perpendicular and six-way seats with the right front seat reclining. In the driveway he said, "How'd you kids like to see all the gadgets?" He started pushing the top up and down, moving the six-way seats back and forth, tilting the steering wheel and turning the stereo tape deck speaker from back to front.

Then the car wouldn't start. Deamis had to push it with his own car.

His father's date was seated on a bar stool of Danny's Hideaway with her legs crossed. She was tall—much taller than his father—and she had long blond hair. Deamis thought she looked just like Crumpet. His father said her name was Muffin.

A waiter led them to a table in the corner. Muffin and Susan Stickwell sat next to each other against the wall.

During dinner Muffin told Deamis about her Negro maid Annabelle. Muffin said, "She has her own personality and everything." She said every morning over breakfast Annabelle told her about her lovers.

Muffin asked Deamis if she could be frank with him. She explained she wasn't at all certain whether to marry his father because Annabelle had threatened to leave her if she moved from her apartment on Park Avenue. "She told me that if I moved from Park Avenue she felt she could no longer hold her head up among her friends in the Negro community."

Deamis's father said, "Say, why don't you two girls go off to the little girls' room so we can have some man talk here?" When they had gone he leaned over to Deamis and said, "Son, Muffin may not be the smartest woman in the world but she's a damn good lay."

Deamis stared at his father. "By the way," his father said, "how's yours?"

Deamis looked down at the tablecloth. He wasn't sure whether he should say he and Susan Stickwell were having intercourse. He wasn't sure whether she was good or not. He wondered if there was anything in the etiquette book about what to say if he were asked this question.

Finally he said, "She's average."

His father didn't answer. He watched Susan Stickwell as she and Muffin came out of the ladies' room and walked toward them. As they approached the table, Deamis's father leaned over to him and said, "That's what I figured."

Part Three

•

Deamis went off to Dooton College, in the town of Dooton's Hole on the Connecticut River in the White Mountains.

Legend had it that when the first colonists pushed north up the Connecticut, they—contrary to the advice of the local Indian chief, Powattan—built their settlement on the bank of the hole and were virtually all drowned the following spring when the river flooded. The few remaining settlers sought the aid of the venerable Powattan, who, in a now legendary ceremony, conjured up his native spirits to urge the river to desist from its course of destruction. Miraculously, the river subsided and the frenzied settlers held their own native ceremony, thanking their own spirit and vowing to repay Powattan in kind by building a college on the spot, for the sole purpose of educating the heathen.

Why the name Dooton was chosen, and not Powattan, is

still something that the college historians avoid answering. One local sage was of the opinion that a certain Eliezer Dooton was killed the next winter in an Indian raid, led by none other than Powattan's son. Old Man Dooton's death, it seemed, had followed (by less than a week) the murder of Powattan himself—who was hacked to death in his tent by none other than Dooton's son Trumble—during a drunken argument over a squaw. (Trumble was also rumored to have been an epileptic.) At any rate, in its one hundred ninety-eight years of existence, Dooton had graduated three Indians.

Deamis found himself in the dormitory that was formerly the Dooton Inn, founded in 1801. It was now a special dormitory for freshmen. In the hallway was a portrait of what was believed to be—although it was never identified as such—Powattan, standing stern and bronze and holding a staff. Under the picture was the scribbled graffiti, "The only good Indian is a dead Indian, and that includes the above son-of-a-bitch."

All the freshmen had to wear beanies. They had to eat in a special freshmen dining room. At night they were chased to the football field where, in a torchlight procession, upperclassmen in green and white uniforms taught them Dooton cheers and football songs.

They sat in the bleachers of an open stadium A boy ran out of the darkness painted like an Indian wearing only a leather breechcloth around his waist. He shouted, "I want to hear all your pea-green voices." They all shouted the name of Dooton College.

Afterward they were chased to the center of campus where a truck filled with railroad ties appeared. An upperclassman in a green and white jacket was seated atop the ties. He shouted why in the name of Eliezer Dooton were they all standing around when they were supposed to be building a bonfire for Dooton's first home football game? Someone shouted that building the bonfire was supposed to build fellowship. Someone shouted, "Dooton is a man's school."

Later at night they played hockey in the dormitory hallways, nearly battering down the doors with their sticks. Someone had a record player and a Johnny Mathis Album, and they all sat on the floor, drank beer from cans, smoked cigarettes and listened to:

> "When Sunny gets blue,
> Her eyes grow grey and cloudy . . ."

and talked of whiskey sours, bloody marys, screwdrivers and "tinis"; practiced using words like "neat," "gross," "shitfaced" and "chone"; spoke deferentially of fraternities they weren't yet allowed to join, of places with such exotic-sounding names as Northhampton, South Hadley and Saratoga, of football games and girls back home, of whether or not you wanted your wife to be a virgin, while Deamis thought of Susan Stickwell and how much more he knew than they, because he had already done it.

During the week the freshmen watched upperclassmen playing touch football in the center of campus or studying in the library, where they dangled their feet on desks and dozed. Saturdays they watched alumni who drove up for football games, parked their cars on dormitory lawns, sat on their fenders and ate box lunches and poured drinks from flasks into paper cups. Those Saturday swarms of girls would appear with long, straight hair down to their shoulders, who wore loafers without socks and walked around the campus holding hands with upperclassmen, or who sat on fraternity porches clinking the ice of their drinks and giggling. From their dormitories at night, the freshmen saw those couples turn into fierce, long figures casting grotesque shadows against fraternity windows as music from electric guitars sang out into the night.

Once a week Deamis and Susan Stickwell called each other. Deamis called at midnight, from a phone booth in the hall, when the hallway was quiet, when the hockey game was over, when there were only two operators on the switchboard and he had to wait ten minutes for one to come on the line, while he wondered whether she would be in or not, then for a line to be open to Philadelphia, while he wondered where she was if she weren't in, then for a line to be open to the junior college, while he wondered if she wasn't in should he leave his name, then for a line to her dormitory because he thought the girls on her floor might think he called too often, then for the Negro maid's voice who answered, "I'm sorry, sir, Miss Stickwell is signed out for the evening."

They wrote letters vowing never to separate like Deamis's parents. Susan Stickwell wrote about her roommate whose father was the chairman of the board of the Chase Manhattan Bank, about the girl next door whose father was a major shareholder in General Electric, about the girl down the hall whose uncle was married to a Dupont.

She wrote about the dates she had: "Dear Deamis, Today is Wednesday, last night I was out with a boy from Swarthmore." Or, "Dear Deamis, Today is Saturday, last night I went out with a boy from Haverford." Or, "Dear Deamis, Today is Monday, I just got home from a weekend at Princeton, next week I am going to Penn."

She wrote about the places she had been: "Dear Deamis, Last weekend I was in New York. We went to the Village Vanguard, in Greenwich Village. My date, who I thought was quite mature, tried to take me to the early show. I told him I wouldn't be caught dead at the early show at the Vanguard."

Susan Stickwell visited Deamis at Dooton. She came, late Friday night on the 3:30 train that went on to Montreal, on a weekend when Deamis's roommate had gone home, so she could sleep in his room.

Deamis waited up for her. Long after the hockey game in the hall had ended, he sat on the floor and smoked cigarettes, listened to Johnny Mathis records, and looked out the windows at the lights of fraternities and other dormitories blinking shut one by one.

At three o'clock he went downtown to the taxi stand. It had started to rain. The driver was asleep in the front seat of his cab, his head against the window. Deamis tapped on the glass. The driver lifted his head and rolled down the window. "In this weather ten dollars," he mumbled.

They drove without speaking to the train station. Deamis sat in the front seat. The windshield wipers made soft rhythmic thuds in the darkness.

The station was dirty. There was the clank and groan of trains. They came in from either end, running backward and forward in short bursts. The driver fell asleep, his mouth open.

Deamis heard a whistle. "That's her," mumbled the driver. "She's running late because of the rain."

Deamis jumped out of the cab and raced along the platform. The rain wet his face. He watched the train slowing into the station. He watched the people through

71

the windows. He saw Susan Stickwell. She was holding a small pink suitcase. She was walking toward him very quickly. She was smoking a cigarette.

He ran toward her and took her suitcase with one hand, bent down and put his arm around her with the other, turned her around, and led her to the cab. In the back seat they kissed. He said she must be very tired. She said, "Poor baby."

They got out at his dormitory and looked to see if there was anyone awake, and holding hands, tiptoed up the stairs and down the hallway to his room. In the darkness she stood by the window. Then she went to the bed, sat with her legs crossed and let him remove her stockings.

Afterward Deamis tried to sleep. His bed was small, and her elbow stuck into his chest. Susan Stickwell snored.

In the morning he watched her putting on her stockings. She wore loafers, and they walked around the campus holding hands.

At night they all sat on the floor and listened to Johnny Mathis records and Deamis thought of all the times he had sat there at night listening to Johnny Mathis and thinking of Susan Stickwell, and now she was here with him.

Someone had made a gin punch. Deamis told Susan Stickwell they usually made strong drinks up here so she'd better be careful. Susan Stickwell drank nine cups of punch. Later she said it was too sweet.

When Deamis took her to the train on Sunday the boys in the dormitory went with them. On the way back someone said Susan Stickwell was neat. Someone else said, "She sure can drink." When they found out she had stayed in his room overnight, Deamis was a hero.

They arranged to sneak home for a weekend together. They arranged to stay at Deamis's house because his mother had just left for her trip abroad, having resolved her affairs in the form of a separation agreement that Arthur Abbot's mother claimed was worthy of royalty, the house not included. Susan Stickwell told Deamis to make a duplicate of his back door key and send it to her by registered mail. She made him swear not to tell anyone. She said, "I'd just die if anyone ever knew."

Deamis took the train one damp, grey Friday in October. He imagined Negro waiters in white jackets serving him dinner, and porters making up upper berths. He imagined looking out the window at the scenery. He imagined taking the midnight train from Pennsylvania Station and walking home past Marinaro's and the Guineas, past the friendly lawns and trees, then hearing the ocean and opening the door and smelling his house's special ocean smell and Susan Stickwell there in the living room waiting for him. He imagined walking to the playground Saturday morning with Susan Stickwell holding his arm, passing younger kids playing basketball who recognized him and stopped to watch. He imagined going to a bar with Susan Stickwell Saturday night and ordering a screwdriver or a whiskey sour.

But there were no waiters in white jackets on the train, and there were no porters. The only other person in Deamis's car was an old man in a red checkered lumberjack shirt with a grey stubble beard who was drinking from a bottle in a paper bag. Another bottle rolled under his seat into the aisle and banged against the seats as the train slowed and started. The train moved very slowly. It stopped at all the little towns: Windsor, Springfield, Bellows Falls and Brattleboro. It was difficult seeing the scenery because the windows were grimy and black.

At Springfield, Massachusetts, they changed trains.

Deamis waited outside on the platform Girls he imagined from Smith and Mt. Holyoke stood on the platform holding small blue or white suitcases and carrying paper-back books.

The other train came. A girl sat down next to Deamis. She was reading *Portrait of the Artist As a Young Man.* She looked up at him. "Do you know Stephen Dedalus?" she said. Deamis shook his head. He looked out the window and wondered where Susan Stickwell was at that very moment. It had started to snow.

It was snowing at the station when he stepped off the midnight train. The snow covered the streets and glowed green and red and orange with the changing traffic lights.

Deamis walked from the station past Marinaro's and the Guineas. He walked past the friendly lawns and trees. They seemed to have a chill on them he had never noticed before.

He came to his house. It was black and the iron gates groaned in the wind. He took out his key and felt it melt into the lock.

The hallway was so dark it frightened him. He turned on the light but the darkness didn't go away. He ran upstairs to smell his house's special smell, but it seemed to have vanished since he went away to college.

He decided to take a shower while he waited for Susan Stickwell. He took off his clothes and let them fall to the floor and turned on the water and felt the steam come up like fog. Then the phone rang.

Deamis raced naked into the bedroom. "Hello, Deamis, this is Mrs. Stickwell. Er . . . Susan tried to call you earlier but apparently you had already left."

Mrs. Stickwell said that due to the inclement weather

74

Susan had thought it best not to come home this weekend. Mrs. Stickwell said Deamis could see her when she came home for Thanksgiving. She said it was only three weeks away.

Deamis walked back to the shower. The steam had filled the bathroom like smoke. He picked up his clothes from the floor, flung them into the empty hamper and he thought of standing under the shower for three weeks until Susan Stickwell came home for Thanksgiving.

When he came out he walked to his parents' room and lay down on his parents' bed. He tried to stretch across it from corner to corner as he had when he was a little boy, but he was too big now and his feet and head stuck over the edges.

The next morning he walked to the school playground. The sun was out, and there were tiny puddles on the court. But there was only one small boy playing, and he was too little even to know who Deamis was.

Thanksgiving, Deamis saw Susan Stickwell. She was sitting in the living room with her mother. Deamis saw them through the window when he rang their bell.

Mrs. Stickwell answered the door. "Why, Deamis," she said, "how wonderful to see you. I know you must love it at Dooton." She led him into the living room. Susan Stickwell was seated on the couch. She was wearing stockings and high-heeled shoes. "Well," said Mrs. Stickwell, "I'd better leave you two alone." She smiled, and went out the door.

Susan Stickwell crossed her legs. She said "I have something to tell you, Deamis." She uncrossed her legs. "About that weekend three weeks ago, well, I could have come, but I was with someone." She crossed her legs again. "I think it only fair to tell you, Deamis, I'm having an affair."

Deamis felt his stomach drop. "He's quite a bit older. He's a senior at Columbia. He comes from Grosse Pointe, although his family also maintains residence in Palm Beach. He graduated from the Cranbrook School, and his father is a large stockholder of the Chrysler Corporation."

Deamis felt his stomach drop again. He tried to pick it up but it was rolling on the floor. He saw Mrs. Stickwell peering in through the door. He didn't want Mrs. Stickwell to see him with his stomach on the floor. He wanted her to see him so she would make Susan Stickwell stop telling about her affair.

"His aunt is related to a Mellon," Susan Stickwell said. "In Pittsburgh."

She said, "So you see, Deamis, we're no longer traveling in the same circles. And besides we'll be moving to Connecticut next month because Daddy has recently accepted a new position for considerably more remuneration."

Suddenly Deamis bent over. He tried to cover his mouth with his hands, but it was dripping over them down to the floor. "Deamis," shrieked Susan Stickwell, "I don't know *what* is the matter with you."

Mrs. Stickwell burst into the room. Deamis heard her whispering, "My God, will you get him out of here before he ruins my rug."

76

Then he was standing outside the front door. Mrs. Stickwell was standing next to him. "I think you'd better be going home now, Deamis," she said. "Not that you're not welcome here. I would have Lester speak to you, but I do not think it would be advisable under the circumstances."

Deamis walked outside but he didn't go home. He lurked in the bushes behind her house. He knew Susan Stickwell was going to see *him*. He just wanted to see what he looked like.

Susan Stickwell came out of the house. She was walking to the corner. She was walking very quickly and smoking a cigarette. Deamis realized she was walking to the train station and he felt himself following.

Deamis thought *he* must be coming in on the train, but instead Susan Stickwell stood on the side where the trains ran to New York. The gates closed, the bell rang and soon a train appeared. He watched Susan Stickwell board it. He watched her walk through the cars and sit down in the third car from the front. He realized she was going to New York, and he felt himself following.

The train started, and the conductor came through the cars. Deamis watched him stop at Susan Stickwell's seat. As she reached for her pocketbook he imagined her turning around and seeing him there behind her. He grabbed a newspaper from the seat next to him and held it in front of his face, peering just over it after each stop to make sure she was still there.

Pennsylvania Station. The honking of taxicabs and reflections in store windows. It had started to rain.

Susan Stickwell had walked quickly through the concourse and out along Seventh Avenue. Deamis had to bump through people to keep sight of her. He saw her spurt ahead, throw her arms around a man's neck, saw him bend down and put his arm around her, turn her around and lead her toward the curb. He looked quite a bit older.

Deamis saw him flick his wrist for a taxi and in the same motion open the door for Susan Stickwell and slide in beside her. Deamis raced to find another cab. "Follow that cab," he shouted to the driver. "What cab, buddy?" asked the driver, turning around and looking at him.

"That one," cried Deamis pointing through the front window. "That one making a left turn."

The taxi driver shot in front of a truck, squeezed between a car and bus, nearly sideswiped another taxi, just missed a pedestrian, made a left turn from the center lane, pulled abreast of them in the middle of Thirty-first Street, screeched on his brakes, cutting them off, and honked his horn. Deamis ducked down on the floor so they wouldn't see him. The driver was laughing. "Something wrong buddy?" he said. "I thought maybe you wanted to say hello to your friends."

Their cab stopped in front of a restaurant. A doorman wearing a hat and white gloves opened the cab door. Deamis watched them get out of the cab. They were holding hands. Other couples were entering. They also looked quite a bit older.

As Deamis got out he thought of asking the driver if he drove many people who followed cabs, but he changed his mind. He stared in the front window of the restaurant. The doorman came over and stared at him so he went away.

Across the street was a diner. Food sizzled on the grill and fluorescent lights buzzed on the ceiling. Deamis sat down at the counter and stared through the steam out the window across the street to the restaurant.

A waitress with a puffy, red face, blond hair, and an apron with a button on her shoulder that read "Please Pay When Served" handed Deamis a menu. Deamis saw she had sweat stains under her arms. She wiped her armpits with her apron.

The menu read: "House special: Fresh Jumbo Louisiana Shrimp nestled in a bed of crisp garden lettuce garnished with creamy cole slaw and golden brown french fries."

The waitress lit a cigarette and stood over him. She was wearing perfume that smelled like cherries. "What's your pleasure?" she smiled.

"Hot dog," said Deamis.

"Plain, handsome? Hey, Louie, gimme a naked dog."

"Coffee? Cream and sugar? Hey Louie, and a sweet mulatto."

The waitress brought Deamis's order. She stood in front of him and watched him eating. Deamis tried to see past her out of the window. His stomach dropped every time someone came out the door. Everytime someone came out the door he smelled her cherry perfume.

The waitress said, "Anything else, handsome?"

"No thank you," said Deamis.

An old man came in and sat down next to him. He said something to the waitress that sounded as though he were gargling. The waitress brought him a glass of water. The old man tried to drink it but it spilled down the front of his coat. He made a motion with his second and third fingers.

The waitress handed the old man her cigarette and put it in his mouth. He gargled again. She took the cigarette back, put it in her mouth, lit it and handed it back to the old man. She smiled at Deamis. "Persistent, isn't he?"

She leaned her elbow on the counter, put her face next to Deamis's and whispered, "Some fellas are more persistent than others."

Then he saw them. They were standing outside the restaurant. They were still holding hands. The waitress smiled at him again. She said, "I guess it all depends on how bad you want something."

He saw them walk towards the diner. He felt in his pocket for change. The waitress said, "Are you sure there's nothing I can do for you?" Deamis shook his head. She picked up a straw that lay in a bowl on the counter, slowly peeled off the paper wrapping and slid it into her mouth. She said, "I like straws. They're round and smooth and when you suck them something warm comes out the front."

Deamis had no change. He had no dollar bills. He threw a five-dollar bill on the counter and fled out the door. The side street was narrow. There were square, squat brownstones on either side of the street. Deamis thought he saw them turn into one. There was a light on in the hallway. He thought he saw their silhouettes climbing the stairs. In a third floor window he saw a light go on.

He raced into the building and began to climb the stairs after them. As he stepped into the hallway he heard a door open. A man's voice said, "Hello, handsome."

A man stepped out into the hallway. He wore a pair of trousers and no shirt. He had a drink in his hand. "Say, haven't I seen you around here before?"

"No," said Deamis.

"Sorry 'bout that," said the man. He called inside the open door. "Hey, Randy. Call Uncle. Tell him I've found something beoo-tee-full.

80

Another man came to the door. He had a towel wrapped around his waist. His body was soft and white. He said, "My, he's so tall, and look at his red hair."

Deamis could see inside the room. It was filled with furniture. There were couches, chairs, dressers, an unmade double bed and a Christmas tree with tinsel in the center of the room.

A third man came out. He wore tight white trousers with a wide red belt around his hips. "Hi," he said. "I'm Randy's uncle. What's your name?"

"Deamis."

"Deamis? That's a nice name." He said, "I don't live here. Sometimes I stay over though. I sleep on the couch. It's good for two but not for three."

Randy said, "What do you do, Deamis?"

"I'm a student."

"A student? That's nice."

Randy's uncle said, "Would you like to come inside and have a drink with us, Deamis? Randy's very nice but he's even better in bed."

Deamis said, "No, I . . ." He turned to walk up the stairs.

"I wouldn't go up there if I were you," said Randy. "*He* just went up there, with a girl."

Randy's uncle said, "Girls may like him but I've seen his apartment and he leaves his underwear lying around." He held his nose. "Pee-you."

Deamis went back downstairs. He crossed the street and looked up at the third floor window. The rain wet his face. He saw a shadow at the window, then a second shadow behind it. He saw the first shadow turn and touch the second shadow. Then the light went out. Nothing was left. Only the rain.

Later Deamis heard the slam of a door and the clicking of high-heeled shoes. When he looked up Susan Stickwell was standing by herself at the corner. She was waving for a taxi. Deamis imagined going up to her and saying, "Why Susan, what are you doing here?" and flicking his wrist for a taxi, then opening the door for her and then walking away.

A taxi stopped. He suddenly knew where she was going. He suddenly knew she would be in the third car of the midnight train, and he felt himself following.

He imagined himself walking down the aisle of the train and saying, "Why Susan, what are you doing here? May I join you?" and slipping into the seat beside her. He wrote out in his mind what he would say to whatever answer she gave him. He practiced saying it over and over to himself in the cab and over and over to himself as he walked to the train.

He started from the back of the train, not really looking in the first few cars, half holding his breath as he came closer to the third car, half hoping she wouldn't be there.

He saw her. She had her legs crossed and had a *Mademoiselle* magazine in her lap. She was smoking.

He stepped in front of her and looked down and said, "Hello Susan, mind if I join you?" and sat down beside her and wondered if his voice was shaking because he realized he should have said, "What are you doing here?" before he said "Mind if I join you?" so, quickly, he said it, "What are you doing here?" and wondered if he sounded surprised enough or if he said it too quickly, so she wouldn't have any idea how he had found her.

"Oh," said Susan Stickwell, "what are *you* doing here, Deamis?"

"Me?" said Deamis. "Oh, I was visiting some friends. Some guys from school. They live in the Village. They wanted to go to the Vanguard, but I told them I wouldn't go unless we went to the late show."

"The Village?" said Susan Stickwell. "I know a girl from school who lives in the Village. What are their names? Maybe she knows them. Her father is a senior vice-president of J. Walter Thompson.

"As a matter of fact," said Susan Stickwell, "she and I and another girl whose father is a partner at Dewey & Ballantine were thinking of rooming together next year. Except that we're not completely certain, you know how it is with three, one is always against the other two, like if two of you have dates you have to fix the third one up so she won't feel left out and then her date probably won't like her and they all end up hating the other two. It can make for a lot of friction, you know."

"Did you have a good time tonight?" asked Deamis. He had to pry the words from his tongue. Susan Stickwell laid her head against the back of her seat. She blew smoke out of her nose and her mouth like a dragon. She whispered, almost as a sigh, "Oh, yes."

Deamis felt a bump in his stomach. He raised his hands to his mouth, but the feeling passed. "Deamis," said Susan Stickwell, "I don't understand what is the matter with you."

"Me?" gasped Deamis. "Oh, nothing. Had a little too much to drink tonight, that's all. These friends of mine. . . ." He shook his head. "Gross guys." He took a deep breath. "Say, what did you do tonight?" Susan Stickwell stared at him coldly.

"I went out."

"What did you do?"

"I don't know why you ask so many questions, Deamis."
She laid her head back against the seat and blew more
smoke out of her nose and mouth. She sighed, "I met
Little Ellie." For a moment Deamis thought he had followed the wrong girl. "After dinner we went back to her
house and turned out the light and listened to the rain."

The train started. Susan Stickwell picked up her
Mademoiselle magazine. Deamis waited for her to put it
down and say something. He tried to think of something
to say to her.

Then it was Jamaica Station, and he had to change
trains. He got up and stood for a moment outside her
window. He waved to her, but she was reading her
Mademoiselle so of course she didn't see him.

♟♟♟

When he returned to school he couldn't sleep. Long after
the hockey game in the hall had ended, long after his
roommate had gone to bed he would sit on the floor and
smoke cigarettes and watch the smoke rise to the ceiling
and listen to Johnny Mathis singing and watch the lights of
fraternities and other dormitories blink shut one by one
until only those in hallways and bathrooms remained.

Later he would lie awake in bed listening to his roommate's breathing and waiting for the whistle of the three-
thirty train and remember that rainy night she had come

to school and they had tiptoed to his room, and he would wonder where she was now and about *him* and what they were doing at that very moment and if it was different from what she had done with him. Then he would long for it to be dawn when he knew she would be safely back in her dormitory and whatever *they* had done would be over.

Or he dreamed about her. She was lying on her back. He was on top of her. Her legs were apart. There was nothing between them.

Then he felt the feeling of the dream the next morning. Sometimes the dream-feeling disappeared after breakfast. Other times it hung about him all through the day.

He decided to quit the basketball team. "Just tell me why," said the coach, a white-haired gentleman who wore a suit and a baseball cap backward, and was called Coach.

"I don't know," said Deamis.

"Is it your studies, son?" said Coach, placing a fatherly hand on Deamis's arm. "Remember, son, Dooton is a man's school. We like a boy here who can do more than study."

Deamis said, "If this is a man's school, where are the women?"

"I said a *man's* school, son," said the coach. "There are no women at a man's school."

Deamis said, "How can it be a man's school if there are no women?"

The following week Deamis received a letter from Hemp, who had just been placed on a year's probation following the report of his discovery with the twelve-year-old runaway. The letter said, "Dear Deamis: I am greatly disappointed in you. I had expected more."

Deamis joined a fraternity. He became one of those long

figures casting grotesque shadows through fraternity windows. He learned new words like "moon," "boot," and "blow lunch." He made road-trips to such exotic-sounding places like South Hadley and Northampton, packed into cars with six boys and six-packs to arrive drunk should their dates be "dogs," and waited on yellow and pink couches in dormitory living rooms for timorous girls, who shook hands, waited for their coats to be held, their car doors to be opened and their mouths to be kissed goodnight.

He became used to IDs, to bring-your-owns, to the narrow, winding unlit roads with dotted white and yellow center lines that curved through mountains and towns with one main street and all-night diners serving greasy eggs and muddy coffee; and dozed in back seats between bony shoulders of pimply boys to music from faraway radio stations, that blurred into static and faded into nothing as they drove on and on through the night and the nights.

That June, Deamis's father, who had recently married a woman named Cupcake, moved into her home in New Canaan, Connecticut, and purchased a turquoise-colored Imperial Le Baron, with safeguard sentinel lighting, automatic beam-changer, automatic temperature-control air conditioning, an electronic brain and four-wheel brake skid-control system with electronic sensors, asked Deamis what he thought of the idea of taking a summer job in the warehouse of Cupcake's former husband's business—of which he had recently become president—with the idea of moving into an important managerial position commensurate with his abilities, when he graduated from Dooton.

"You might as well face it, son," his father said, "money buys a lot of cunt in this world."

His father asked Deamis to visit their home in New Canaan for the weekend to discuss it. He said it would also be a good chance for him to get to know Cupcake. "Wait till you see her," his father said. "You'll come all over yourself."

Cupcake was sitting on the veranda, with her legs crossed, painting her toenails. She was tall, much taller than his father, and she had long blond hair. Deamis thought she looked just like Muffin.

During lunch Cupcake asked Deamis if he would like to see the urn with her former husband's ashes. "Everything happened so fast with your father I didn't have a chance to get rid of them," she said.

After lunch Cupcake showed Deamis the neighborhood. They walked past a house with the name Stickwell written on a sign on the lawn. A young man was raking leaves.

The door opened and Mrs. Stickwell came out. She said, "Mark, I told you to be careful of my flower beds." Then she saw Deamis. She said, "Why Deamis, whatever are you doing in this neighborhood? I think it only fair to tell you that Susan is already engaged."

Then she said to Cupcake, "Why, we must be neighbors. . . ." She said, "I don't know how you feel about the subject, but Lester and I have always looked upon ourselves as very fortunate to be able to live in this beautiful, refined community, where people have the right kind of values." She said, "Lester and I both feel breeding is every bit as important as riches."

Before Deamis left, Cupcake told him that any son of his father's was a son of hers but would he please not mention to anyone whenever he visited them that he was four-thirteenths Jewish.

The next week Deamis received a letter from Susan Stickwell. The letter said,

> "Dear Deamis, I think it only fair to tell you that my name will no longer be Susan Stickwell but Susan Stickwell Thistle. I am engaged to Thomas Thistle II. He is quite a bit older. His uncle is related to a Duke. In North Carolina. From a previous marriage, Thomas has two children named Wilbur age eight, and Winnifred age six. We are expecting to have one ourselves some day in the not too distant future named Alice or Alden. As the children both love animals we also are planning to acquire two turtles, which we will name Minnie and Montie, a dog, to be named Harold, a cat to be named Samuel, three goldfish to be named Jake, Pearl and Ruby and two hamsters whose names have not been determined as of yet. Thomas hasn't been to work for the past two weeks because of his sinuses. Sincerely Yours, Susan Stickwell Thistle."
>
> P.S. I always told you I wanted hamsters.

Deamis carefully folded the letter. He thought of Susan Stickwell, and their star. He remembered her saying that day after school, "It's so close, you can just reach up and touch it. Would you reach up and catch me a star if I asked you to, Deamis?" He unfolded the letter and tried to read it again, but he stumbled over the Thistle and could go no farther.

Deamis began work in Cupcake's former husband's warehouse. It was on Cliff Street at the foot of the Brooklyn Bridge. All the buildings on Cliff Street were warehouses. Long trucks were parked on both sides of the black tar streets.

Deamis had to take the subway to Fulton Street. The men in the subway all carried boxlike briefcases and *Wall Street Journals* and scurried past him out of the dank, dark station.

The foreman of the warehouse was named Monty McGuire. He was lean and dark with a razor-thin mustache. He said he had three boys working under him. He called them numero uno, numero dos, numero tres. Numero uno was named Lion. He was bald with a red, round face and a broque, and he called Deamis, Daymus. Lion told Deamis his daughter cut his hair once a month so he saved a buck by not going to the barber. He said he used to be a Brooklyn Dodger fan before they moved away but now he didn't follow baseball anymore because it had gone too commercial.

Numero dos was Henry Stolina. Henry had grey hair slicked back and parted in the middle and wore a pencil behind each ear. His back was bent like a comma. He told

Deamis he was living proof that this was backbreaking work.

Henry Stolina told Deamis he had been working in the warehouse for thirty-five years and could give him a history of every nook, cranny and piece of dirt. He told Deamis he had been there when the warehouse had been used to package furs and hides and then when it had become a tool and die factory, and that he had known John Older, the former owner who had sold the warehouse to Cupcake's former husband for twenty-five thousand dollars. "Me and Johnny-boy, we were like brothers," said Henry Stolina.

Lion said that John Older had probably told Cupcake's former husband, "For twenty-five thousand dollars, we'll also throw in Henry Stolina."

Numero tres was a black man named Phurphey. Henry Stolina said Phurphey had come just a few months before Deamis but that he didn't know very much.

The warehouse had six floors. Each floor was covered with sawdust. There was an elevator with an iron grate door that Henry Stolina ran. Henry Stolina told Deamis he was the only one permitted to drive it. He said he had driven it for John Older, who was the best owner the warehouse had ever had. "And that includes anyone you may be related to."

Henry Stolina told Deamis that if he were smart he would watch out for Monty. He said that Monty was very strong and mean and warned Deamis never to cross him. He said Monty would make it tough on Deamis if he ever thought Deamis was trying to take his job because he was the boss's son and Monty was nothing but a dumb Irishman who looked like a Polack.

Monty showed Deamis to his locker. He said each man

had his own locker. He said that was one of the benefits they had without the union.

The lockers were on the second floor. There were rows of them. The room was dark and the floor was torn linoleum. At the end of the locker room was a washroom. It had a sink and a toilet but no toilet paper.

Monty told Deamis he could wear the special warehouse uniform or he could bring his own clothes like dungarees, as he chose. He said there was a pair of overalls and special warehouse sneakers in his locker. He said Deamis could change into his overalls there in the morning or into his dungarees, as he wished.

He told Deamis he would show him the layout. On each floor there were cartons. They were piled against the wall, fat, yellow, and of different sizes. Each carton had numbers written on it with a line between the numbers. Monty said it was called a slash line. Monty said, "The most important thing is to know your inventory." He said the cartons were the inventory. He said all the cartons together were the line.

Monty told Deamis he could begin working up on the sixth floor. He said Henry would take him up in the elevator. He said, "When you get a little experience we'll let you come down and unload with us."

The sixth floor was hot. It smelled of sawdust. The windows were grey. Henry told Deamis his job was to make up packages and put them in little cardboard cartons and fill them with sawdust so they wouldn't break in transit, and then put the little cartons into a big carton. He said to make sure, when Deamis closed the big cartons, to put a heavy tape across the sides which said: FRAGILE, HANDLE WITH CARE.

Each morning after Deamis changed into his uniform

Henry took him in the elevator up to the sixth floor and left him there. Deamis stared at the cartons and at the grey window and at the sawdust on the floor and peered down the elevator shaft watching the chain of the elevator shake as it went down.

During the morning he stared at the windows of warehouses across the street and wondered if people were packing cartons on their sixth floors. Or he would walk over to the elevator and watch the chain to see if it were moving and wonder on what floor the elevator was stopping.

At noon, when the lunch whistle blew, Deamis waited by the elevator for Henry to come for him. Henry told Deamis Monty had told him he would be allowed to unload with them on the first floor as soon as he proved he could be trusted.

Sometimes a truck would be sitting in the ramp when Deamis came down for lunch. The backs of the trucks were filled with cartons and the men would climb over them as though they were snowdrifts and lift them up on their shoulders, and march out with them one at a time.

There were two trucking companies that brought in the line. One was run by a man named Willie who wore a hat with a green feather in it, smoked a cigar that stuck out of the side of his mouth, and left the two top buttons of his shirt open showing bushy grey hair on his chest. He stood at Monty's desk and joked with Monty while the men unloaded. Henry Stolina told Deamis Willie used to take out Monty's wife before Monty married her, that's why they were such good friends.

The other trucking line was the Big Jackie Tibbet Express Inc., which was written on the sides of their trucks. The Big Jackie Tibbet Express Inc. had two drivers, Big Jackie and Prince. They both wore tight jerseys with short sleeves and had tattoos all over their arms. Deamis thought they were twins.

"Naw, just good friends, kiddo," Big Jackie said. He said that he and Prince had grown up together, gone to school together, broken windows together, stolen fruit together and gotten lots of ass together. Big Jackie said, "Hey, kiddo, how old were ya when youse copped ya first piece of ass?"

"Sixteen," Deamis lied. Big Jackie started to laugh. He said, "Hey Prince, did ya hear that? He says he was sixteen when he copped his first snatch."

Deamis was about to say maybe it was seventeen when Big Jackie said, "Shit, we wuz fuckin' when youse wuz still in diapers. I wuz fuckin' a friend of my sister's when I was eleven and Prince here he fucked a friend of hers when he was twelve." He said, "I guess that shows how much guys who go to college know."

The men ate lunch together on the ramp where the trucks came in and dangled their feet and looked across at the Brooklyn Bridge. They all ate together except Monty. Henry Stolina said Monty liked to eat at his desk by himself because he read *The Wall Street Journal*, which he kept in his lunchbox and didn't want anyone to know. Henry Stolina said sometimes Monty read *The Wall Street Journal* when he pretended he was making out bills of lading. He said he knew for a fact that Monty had money in Chrysler Corporation. He said, sometimes during lunch Monty snuck over to the market to check on his stocks when he thought no one would see him.

Henry Stolina told Deamis about the robbery they had

had two years ago. He said, "They shit on Monty's desk." He said, "If Monty was so smart he would have put toilet paper in the washroom like I told him."

Each day one of the men went to the Italian grocery around the corner to buy hero sandwiches and beer. Big Jackie said, "It's the only place where you can get meat, eggs and potatoes for thirty cents. Kielbasa, hard-boiled eggs and a bag of potato chips. Har. Har."

He nudged Deamis. "Hey, kiddo," he said, ya ever do it in the ass?" He looked over at Prince and whispered to Deamis, "He's an asshole bandit."

Prince laughed. He said, "Yeah, I learned when I did time. CCW, little shit, but they gave me a year. I never took it though. Hell," he said, "they all do it in the can. You know, they get some skinny worthless kid, he'd get himself mixed up with some buck nigger for protection who'd give him a jump a few times and pass him around."

Prince lit a cigarette. He said, "Yeah, I remember my first. I was head man in the cell. I was only seventeen but they saw I was tough and they made me head man, what the hell, I cooperated with the screws. I was in charge of giving out medicine. This hillbilly was in there, he was about thirty-five with thin blond hair and he says to me, 'I got to have some Demerol.' I said, 'I can't do it.' He said, 'I'll suck your dick.' I said, 'You got to let me fuck you.' He said, 'Sure.'

"So that night we went into the bathroom, I told one of the guys to keep guard and I took a picture of my wife out of my wallet and I kept looking at her when I did it. I had to keep looking at her and then there was some noise and it was the goddamn screw. He was all right, he didn't do nothin' but give me a lecture. He said he had a boy seventeen himself and the last thing he would have liked was for him to be fucking assholes.

"But ya know, after that I did it alot. All the time I could. Even now I still do it. Not with men. I got this friend of my old lady's next door, she can take a dick with the best of them. Got her once when the old lady was in the next room. My wife don't like it though. I think her asshole is too small."

While Deamis worked at the warehouse he lived at a hotel on the Upper West Side. The name of the hotel was the Acupulco. Deamis found it through an ad in *The New York Times* which said: "newly reconditioned rooms from ninety-five dollars and up." The manager told him that since he had placed the ad he had received calls from all over the world asking for reservations. He said he would give Deamis a break, however, because he was a student.

The lobby of the Acupulco was linoleum and smelled of wax and ammonia. The elevator skipped floors. Two of the numbers on the buttons had been rubbed out and Deamis was never certain whether he was pushing one or three, or two or four.

He was given a room on the third floor. He walked down cavernous hallways with garbage cans at every corner and radio sounds and cooking smells that seeped under doors and through transoms. The room faced Broadway. The walls were light blue, and a picture hung above his bed. At night he went to sleep to the flickering marquees of movie theaters, the belching of buses, the whine of garbage trucks, the clang of fire engines, the whoosh of the express flying into ⁻the tunnel like the wind, the screech of the local as it stopped, and the TV of the lady next door.

The people at the Acupulco were old. They had brittle bodies, and shuffled about in bedroom slippers. The men had unshaven faces with grey stubble. The women had cheeks with creases filled with rouge, and lipstick on the corners of their mouths. They all knew each other. They sat in the lobby and talked. They were there in the morning when Deamis came down for work, and they were there in the evening when he went up to his room. On warm days they bundled up in overcoats and perched on benches on Broadway like flocks of birds. At night they stood in front of newsstands waiting for the *Daily News*. Sometimes Deamis stood near them and tried to hear what they were saying, but when they saw him they became silent, so he felt he had to go away.

Every morning he woke to the lady-next-door's clock radio. He heard her singing:

> "When Irish eyes are smiling,
> And the world is bright and gay . . ."

in a high squeaky voice.

Once he saw her. Her door was open and she was sitting on her bed, wearing a ratty black bathrobe. She had white legs with blue veins. Once he woke up to her phone ringing. He heard her saying, "Yes, yes, you're coming this Sunday." She started to scream. She said, "No goddamn you, no, I don't care if I never see you again." He heard

96

her slam down the phone and heard her saying over and over, "Goddamn you, goddamn you!"

Then he heard her crying. He imagined her sitting on her bed in her black bathrobe. He wished her clock radio would go on so that he wouldn't be able to hear her.

Every other Sunday his father called him from Connecticut to ask him how he was getting along in the business world. "Don't forget what I told you about the pussy," he said.

Every Sunday, his mother, who had recently returned from a trip to South America and was currently on a tour of the Greek Islands, called him from a different island. She said that since she was calling long distance she would confine herself to essentials. "Deamis?" she would say when he answered, "Good morning. Here are last week's closing stock prices that should be of concern to you: Westinghouse, fifty-three and one-half, up an eighth. Standard Oil of New Jersey steady at forty-four. IBM down five to 354. AT&T up a half to sixty-three. That concludes this morning's report. Good morning, Deamis."

July came and with it came the heat. On the sixth floor the heat crawled out of the corners, rubbed along the dirty grey windows, and wrapped itself around the fat yellow cartons.

The men worked at the warehouse in their undershirts. They sweated down their chests and arms and wiped their foreheads with the back of their palms. When Deamis lifted his arms, the heat trickled into his eyes and down his cheeks and across his upper lip, onto his tongue and under his clothes.

He began to dread going to the warehouse each morning. He dreaded going down into the hot subway and crowding against people and their smells and women's straps and shaven underarms. He dreaded getting off at the Fulton Street stop. He dreaded men with their boxlike briefcases and *Wall Street Journal*s, scurrying past him in the dark, dank station. He dreaded walking to the warehouse where the long red trucks sat on the soft black tar streets.

He dreaded going to the dark second floor with the torn linoleum and putting on his overalls and special warehouse shoes. He dreaded the elevator and its iron grate door. He dreaded Henry Stolina with his slicked-back hair, part in the middle, pencil behind his ears, and bent back.

He dreaded the sixth floor. After Henry let him off he stood at the edge of the elevator shaft and peered down it and watched the chain move until the elevator had gone to the first floor and the chain stopped. He spent the morning counting the minutes until lunch. He spent the afternoon counting the minutes until closing.

In the summer, bums appeared under the bridge like sores. Sometimes they appeared in the morning when the men came to work. Other times they came out at noon when the men ate lunch. Sometimes they were there in the evening when the men went home.

They would lie on the sidewalk in the cool of the archway, dirty, smelling, and grisly-unshaved like giant scabs. Monty called them "scum-a-the-earth." From the sixth floor Deamis would hear the smash of glass against

98

the pavement and see Monty running after them, scream-
ing, "Ya goddamn scum-a-the-earth."

Once a policeman tried to wake the bums who were
sleeping under the bridge. He poked at them with his
nightstick, and held out his stick for them to grab. The
bums yelled. They swung their arms at the policeman. The
policeman hit one on the head with his stick. It made a
soft crunch sound. The bum sank to the ground. There was
blood on the pavement. Later an ambulance came. The
siren pierced the heat like a needle.

Every day after lunch Phurphey came up to the sixth
floor to work with Deamis. He said he would teach
Deamis the ropes. Phurphey said his friends called him
Kingsnake. He called Deamis Muldoon.

He said he would teach Deamis the ropes. "First lesson,
Muldoon, you line up all the little cartons next to each
other and then fill them with sawdust before you put any
of them into the big cartons. Then you close all the big
cartons before you put FRAGILE, HANDLE WITH CARE tape
on any of them. See," he said, "why make trouble for
yourself, Muldoon?"

While they packed cartons, Phurphey and Deamis talked.
Phurphey told Deamis his life story. He said he was
originally from the islands. "Born and bred." He said,
"You want to have a good time, man, that's where you
go." Phurphey said his sister still lived down there and that
if Deamis ever wanted to go there for a vacation he should
tell him and he would give him her address.

Phurphey said he was thinking of leaving the warehouse
pretty soon because he had something better he was lining
up, if he got the right breaks. He said he didn't want to say
what it was yet because he was still working on it and if he

did it might spoil it, but as soon as it came through he would give Deamis all the details. He said, "Who knows, Muldoon, maybe it's you. Maybe the white man is going to change the Kingsnake's luck."

Phurphey said that even if it didn't work out he wouldn't work in the warehouse all summer long because of the summer basketball league. He said, "That's my game. Got a deadly eye." Deamis said, "I play basketball, too." Phurphey said, "You watch me play, Muldoon, maybe you can pick up a few pointers."

Phurphey explained that even if he quit the warehouse tomorrow he would still be solvent because he had VISTAs living with them. "You know, those white kids who come to help Negroes better themselves?"

Deamis said, "What's wrong with the way you are?"

Phurphey said, "I don't know. But they pay us four dollars a day for each of them. They stay with us for eight weeks and then we get a new batch. They call us foster parents. Sheeit, all we do is just move some of our kids in with us and put the VISTAs in the back room." He said, "Sheeit, they even pay you if they're deselected in the middle."

Phurphey said that the job at the warehouse was just interim anyway since he had been let go from his last job a few months before and needed something to tide him over. He explained that before he worked at the warehouse he had had a job in a garage parking cars, but that he had been fired. "They said it was stealing," said Phurphey, "but it wasn't. It was tastin'."

He said, "See, I used to work the night shift, and when business was slow I'd take a car for a spin around the block, you know, to keep the battery up, like.

"Well, there was this Jag, this long, sleek thing that was sittin' there for over two months without no one ever even noticin' her. I'd see her there every night, way in the back of the garage, sittin' there quiet behind four or five other cars, lookin' so sad 'cause no one ever showed her the slightest interest.

"Well, it got so every night I'd walk over to the Jag and look in at the speedometer just to see if anyone had taken her out during the day but I knew the answer before I ever poked my head inside, it was the same every time.

"You know it got so bad I couldn't think of nothin' else but that Jag? I'd be thinkin' 'bout her during the day when I was home with the wife and I'd come in the evening and first thing I'd go over to her and see if she was the same, without any more mileage. It got so I could feel her staring at me with those sad headlights and I could almost hear her engine purring to me as I came up close, and her body shake when I ran my hand 'cross the hood.

"Then finally, one night it happened. There was only two of us, me and this white cat who hadn't been there but a couple of weeks, so I said, "Look man she really wants it bad, I got to do my piece." I waited till it was late and I knew there was no customers, and one by one I start moving all the other cars away so we'd have a clear path, you know, and I go over and I touch her (just the tip of the door handle), and I open it real gentle and run my hand over the top of her smooth dashboard and slip in behind the wheel into that soft seat and stick the key in and feel it fit smooth into the ignition and I say, 'OK, girl, now we're going to ride,' and I turn it on, and Lord if she doesn't start right up as though she had been panting for this moment.

101

"I glide it up the ramp and let out the clutch real slow and easy so as not to hurt her 'cause you know how it is after they haven't been used to it for a while and ease her down into the street, and we're in first, the gear shift down next to me on the floor, and I slip it into second and whisper, 'Now I'm going to let you out, I'm going to let you run,' and I can almost hear her sighing back to me, 'Yeah, Kingsnake, I'm ready,' she's saying, 'I'm ready.'

"So I ease her over to the West Side Highway and I slide over into the left-hand lane and get ready to let her cut loose. I throw her into fourth and I say, 'Now do your stuff.' And damn, she starts to purr, she starts to moan, she starts to roar, and we're flying now and she's roaring so smooth I want to cry. I can feel her lights looking back at me and saying, 'Thank you, thank you, Kingsnake, you're giving me more pleasure tonight than I can ever remember.'

"So there we are ridin' up the West Side Highway, the windows down, the wind blowin' in my face, tears down my cheeks I'm so proud, past that big Yale truck that's stuck up there right over the road, past those new buildings that stick up so thin like matchboxes with those lights twinkling, and further up there on the left, that big mother-fuckin' George Washington Bridge all lit up green and white and yellow, and I beep the horn so everyone can know how happy we are, beep, beep, beep and like when I touch her horn it's like I'm touchin' a nerve, and we take off even faster and I'm thinkin', should I take her all the way up to Connecticut or over to the Harlem River Drive and then back downtown down the East Side Drive? So I let up on the gas and I feel her pleading with me because she thinks I'm going to turn around, and I say, 'Listen since this is just the first time, we got plenty other nights together, we are going to get to know each other real fine, you and me.' Next thing I know she gives a little cough as though I've taken my foot up too quick and then next thing I know, we're slowing down, and I look down at the gas, and—yeah—you guessed it, we're out of gas.

"Well I pull it over and we're sittin' down near the boat basin and I'm waiting for the po-leece to arrive because I know they ain't goin' to see no nigger drivin' a car like that without they want to know where's the registration, and I say, 'We've had it, you and me, the man is goin' to fry my ass,' and then I hear the siren, they was comin' already.

"Well that was about six months ago," Phurphey said. "Then I came to this job." He shrugged his shoulders. "What can you do, man?"

The next week Phurphey told Deamis to congratulate him, he was leaving. He said his other job had come through and that Friday was his last day.

"Man, don't look so sad, Muldoon. Sure, we had some good times, but sheeit, this ain't a job for no man, black or white. Sheeit, Muldoon," said Phurphey. "At the end of the summer you're goin' back to college, right? But me, if I stay here I ain't got sheeit. Look, Muldoon," he said, "I'll tell you what. You 'member those VISTAs I told you 'bout? Well, we got this new batch last week and they're havin' this welcome party tomorrow night. Maybe you want to come."

Phurphey added, "Look, I'll write down the address. It's in the Bronx. Near Boston Road and 166th Street. You take the IRT to 149th Street and then take the Third Avenue El. When you get out you look for a sign that says 'Millionaires' Club.' Then you just walk up the hill, past the playground, turn left and keep walking past the alley, and just look for my green door. Get it?"

That night Deamis had a dream. He dreamed he was on the sixth floor, and it was closing time, but the elevator didn't come for him. He pushed the button. He pushed it again and again. He watched the chain but it remained still.

He started to pound the wall of the elevator shaft. He started to scream. Finally he saw the chain moving, and the elevator appeared. Henry Stolina was standing inside but he didn't open the door. He was staring at Deamis and shaking his head and saying, "Thirty-five years, I've been going up and down here for thirty-five years. I've been going up and down for thirty-five years.

"Open the door, Henry," pleaded Deamis. "Open the door and let me in. Henry, please open the door."

Deamis started to bang on the cage of the elevator. "Henry," he shrieked, "open the door, please open the door." But Henry just stared at him, shook his head and said, "Thirty-five years, thirty-five years," and then the elevator started going down and Deamis stood watching the chain moving, and then the chain was still.

Part Four

•

It was evening when Deamis came out of the subway at 149th Street and walked up the rickety wooden platform for the Third Avenue El. Lights of stores flickered below. Crowds of black men stood at corners. They wore green pants and orange shirts holding transistor radios to their ears.

The El rolled in, a short brown train with squat, square cars. The doors groaned closed and they rolled out. They ran level with the tops of red-brown tenements that seemed to sag on each other. In the window of one Deamis saw a man in an undershirt. He was sitting on the window-sill and puffing a cigarette.

At 166th Street Deamis got out. He walked past the dingy wooden token booth, out of the chipped green swinging doors and down the grey metal steps to the sidewalk. There, between the black legs of the El, sat a bed, two mattresses, and wicker chairs. Barefoot black children in torn white underpants swarmed over them. The

107

El rumbled overhead. The stores were boarded up with wood and metal bars. Through the bars of the window Deamis saw the words 'Millionaires' Club.'

Deamis turned and walked up the hill. He passed a cement playground and a vacant lot filled with beer cartons and broken bottles. He turned left, past an alley. Next to it was a green metal door. Deamis banged on it. It opened, and Phurphey said, "Man where you been? I didn't think you were comin'."

Little children rushed to the door behind Phurphey and crawled up Deamis's arms and legs. "Hey you kids," shouted Phurphey, "You leave him alone. He ain't no VISTA."

A round brown woman with rich, milk-chocolate arms wobbled to the doorway and said, "What the hell," noticed Deamis and said, "Oh, pleased to meet you I'm sure," turned, and walked back inside. Phurphey said, "That's my wife, Rhoda."

Phurphey led him into the living room. It was small and dim, filled with two couches and a large television set that was showing American Bandstand, and more little children lying on the floor watching it with their mouths open.

In the middle of the children sat a young man with blond hair. Phurphey said, "Hey Harry, this here's Muldoon." He said to Deamis, "This here's Harry, he's one a them VISTAs I was tellin' you about."

Harry stood up and nodded his head. He said, "I'm awfully pleased to meet you, Mr. Muldoon."

A white sheet was hanging at the corner of the room like a curtain, separating the living room from the bedroom. A young man came out from behind the sheet. He was very

108

short and wore thick glasses, and he had a large, curled red mustache. Phurphey said, "This here is Martinez. He's our other VISTA."

Deamis stared at him. He was staring at Martinez's thick glasses. "Boomer!" he gasped.

Boomer laughed, "Hey cat, what's happening?" He said, "Man, you sure have grown. I guess you always were pretty tall."

"Boomer," gasped Deamis. "How are you? How are your parents? Where have you been? What have you been doing? What's happened to you? How is your father?"

"Oh, man," scowled Boomer, "don't bother me with that shit. We're not on the same wavelength. I've got me a pad down on Westchester Avenue with my chick. Her name's Juanita. We're livin' common law."

Phurphey said, "Hey, you know each other?"

"Yeah, man," said Boomer, "we're home boys." He said to Deamis, "Look, cat, I'm organizing here. I'm organizing the brothers and sisters. I've got about thirty people in the community who are ready to join us. We're thinking of going statewide, or maybe even national." He added, "Look, we're having a party tonight. Some people are coming who I want you to meet. They're very important. WS might be coming also. He's the most beautiful white cat you've ever seen."

They ate supper, Deamis, Boomer, Harry, Phurphey and Rhoda, sitting around a small table in the kitchen. The kitchen was hot and steamy. Food bubbled on the stove, and a portable record player on the refrigerator played:

Phurphey's little children, who were still sitting on the floor of the living room watching television, stood up and shook their little bodies to the music as though they were doing calisthenics.

At the back of the kitchen was a door. It was open and Deamis could see inside. There was a stone floor and pipes running along the walls and the ceiling. Boomer said, "That's the back room, where James and I and Harry sleep." He said, "I put a chinning bar in there for the kids. I also taught them to play catch in the alley."

A young man came through the back-room door. He nodded to Boomer and to Harry and to Deamis, and sat down at the table. Phurphey said to Deamis, "This here is James. He's my eldest." James looked up at Deamis and nodded again.

After dinner people started arriving for the party. There were black men in green pants and orange shirts, black girls in short red and orange dresses with bright-colored stockings and white VISTA boys and girls in dungarees with long unkempt hair and pimples, who smiled continuously and said "Hello, Mr. Phurphey," and "Hello, Mrs. Phurphey," and who sat on the floor tickling Phurphey's little children and crawling on their hands and knees giving piggyback rides.

Phurphey turned on the record player:

"If you want someone to play with,
Go find yourself a toy. . . ."

They all started to dance. The black men danced with the white VISTA girls. The white VISTA boys danced with the black girls. Everyone was dancing. They all bumped into each other.

Deamis stood in a corner and watched everyone dancing.

Phurphey and James were dancing with girls with straggly blond hair down to their waists. The record played:

"Baby my time is too expensive,
And I'm not your little toy."

Phurphey smiled when he danced. James closed his eyes and puffed on a cigarette.

Rhoda said to Deamis, "We got Gordon's, and Johnny Walker Red, and if you want somethin' with it there's some juice in the kitchen."

A tall, light-skinned Negro woman walked up to Deamis. She said, "You a VISTA too?" Phurphey stopped dancing and said, "Sheeit, he ain't no VISTA, he works with me."

The woman said, "Oh yeah? Well he don't look like no VISTA."

Phurphey said to Deamis, "That's Alice. She lives around the corner on Franklin Avenue. Her husband, Obie, he's my partner."

A VISTA boy came up and danced with Alice.

Deamis watched Alice dancing. He watched her shaking her long body. Phurphey said, "The bitch thinks she's cute because she's yellow."

Deamis saw Rhoda dancing, shaking her round, fleshy body. "Just make yourself at home Deamis darlin'," she said to him as she danced by.

Another VISTA danced with Alice. Another VISTA danced with Rhoda. Phurphey's children, standing behind the sheet in torn white underpants, peeked out at the dancers and shook their little bodies.

Deamis saw Boomer. He was sitting on the floor in the middle of a group of VISTAs. He had pulled up a corner of the rug and was writing on the floorboards with a piece of chalk. "Hey cat," he called to Deamis, "come on over. I want you to see this."

Deamis sat down on the floor next to Boomer. He looked down at what Boomer had drawn on the floor. There were maps and charts and diagrams. Boomer explained that the VISTAs were trying to organize the community to rise up against their oppressors. He said, "We're going to give the black man back his dignity that the white man has robbed him of. That's WS's philosophy. WS says that dignity is the essence of humanism. He's trying to get some cats up on Park Avenue to fund us. After the struggle is all over he says he's going back to Mexico to live with real people." Boomer said, "After the struggle is over, me and my chick are going to live with real people too, on Westchester Avenue."

Boomer leaned over and whispered to Deamis, "Look, cat, I may be able to get you into the program." He said there was a sudden opening because Harry had recently been deselected. Boomer said, "He didn't relate."

Boomer said, "Look, cat, just wait for me over there in the corner to finish with these people. Then I'll see what I can do to help you."

While Deamis waited for Boomer he drank some Johnny Walker Red and watched Skinny Alice dancing. She was wiggling her long body and running her tongue over her lips and smiling at him.

Phurphey walked up to him. "That Skinny Alice sure got eyes for you, Muldoon," he said. "Uh, oh," he added,

"That's trouble over there for certain." He pointed to a man wearing a green derby who was standing in the corner snapping his fingers to the music. "That's Obie," Phurphey said. He shook his head. "That cat just don't do his homework."

Phurphey called over to him. "Obie," he said, "this here's my man Muldoon." Obie stopped snapping his fingers. He said to Deamis, "Man, you take JFK, LBJ, any a them smart cats and put them up against me on Boston Road and see how good they do."

Boomer walked over to them. He said to Phurphey, "Hey, man, what do you say about Deamis taking Harry's place in the program when he leaves?"

Phurphey stared down at Boomer. He stared up at Deamis. He said "Muldoon, you want to be a VISTA?" He stared back down at Boomer. "Well, sheeit," he said to Deamis, "for the money you pay at that rattrap hotel you'd be better off stayin' here. For four dollars a day you get all the food you can eat. Sheeit, that warehouse ain't no place for any man."

Boomer said to Deamis, "See, cat, I told you I could help you."

Phurphey went and danced with Skinny Alice. Then Boomer danced with her. The record was playing:

"Deep down inside of me,
Just forget your foolish pride."

Deamis watched her. She was holding a drink in her hand while she danced. He watched her throw her head back and laugh.

Skinny Alice walked over to Deamis and handed him her

113

glass. She put her arms on his shoulders, wiggled her long body into his and swayed from side to side against him to the music. She said, "I saw you talkin' to Obie over there. He just plain mean now. See, my girlfriend Leslie used to live wif me, I hadn't seen her for a long time, you know? and I bumped into her, we used to go to school together, go round boostin', you know, when we were kids? and she'd just busted up wif her ole man so I said, 'Hey, Leslie, come on in wif me,' you know, like a wife-in-law, 'cause she used to know Obie too, even though I didn't know this, see, and she said, 'Cool' 'cept I'd come home at night like at twelve-thirty and I'd want to sleep, you know, and she'd be playin' records all night—so I said, 'Honey, you got to do somepin' 'bout those records' and she said 'Sure, honey.' and next night the same thing—so one night I said, 'Girl, you just get your stinky ass right outa here' and Obie says, 'Now what are you gettin' mad at honey?' and I said, 'You can get your ass outa here too you motha-fucka."

"See, 'fore Obie, I had this old man Chuckie he was really cool, but see I was younger, you know? he was the one taught me how to boost, you know like you go into some place like Sears and you take three dresses to try on and you fold one over your arm and leave the other two, see, so the lady can't do nothin' cause she thinks you only got two and then you say somepin' like you don't want it cause it's too small or somepin' and you just walk out wif the other one under your coat, like sheeit I got me my whole wardrobe just boostin', you know, all knits and furs and worsteds until that motha-fucka Cooley busted into my room and stole it all. I got so good at it I never got picked up 'cept once in Woolworth's of all places, me and Leslie were in there and she had her two kids you know? and I didn't think they'd catch on, Lord, I cried, I said it was my first time, but that detective there he was smart, he saw Leslie runnin' back toward me all the time and he saw I was eyein' him and he was eyein' me at the same time, you know out of the corner of our eyes cause I said to myself, he looks like a store detective you know? so what he did was he went through the check-out line so I thought maybe he's a customer and then he grabbed me, I had it up here and in my pockets and under my dress and in my pocketbook, you know, and when I said it was my first time he said, 'Uh uh, girl. You're too good for it to be the first time.' "

Skinny Alice shook her head. She slid her arms along Deamis's shoulders around his back, put her face against his, and wiggled her long body into him. He smelled her breath of gin and heard the music:

"Tell it like it is,
   Don't be ashamed, let your conscience be your guide."

He felt her lips, cool and warm on his neck, and thought he heard her murmur, "Yeah, Deamis, that's how it is."

Deamis moved into Phurphey's house, into the back room with Boomer. They slept in a double-decker bed, next to another double-decker bed, where James and three of

Phurphey's little children slept. James slept in the top bunk. The little children slept in the bottom bunk. They slept toe to head and head to toe.

The back room was hot. They all slept naked. In the mornings it was difficult for Deamis to wake up because of the heat. He half heard the little children in the bathroom, half heard them urinating in the toilet bowl, flushing the toilet, running the water in the faucet, then the music from the record player on the refrigerator and the water bubbling on the stove.

Boomer told Deamis he expected him to get up early each morning so that he would be ready to go with him when he went out to organize. "You see," said Boomer "organization is the essence of revolution."

Boomer explained that when they organized, it was very important that Deamis wore the right clothes. Boomer wore dungarees and a white T-shirt and carried a boxlike briefcase like the men at the Fulton Street stop. He said the reason he dressed as he did was so that he could relate better to people.

Boomer said, "That was Harry's main trouble. He didn't relate."

Boomer led Deamis into the red and brown brick tenements under the El. The hallways of every building smelled of urine and dried whiskey and were strewn with broken bottles. Boomer would go into the buildings and up the stairs, knock on doors and say, "Excuse me, sir or madam, but do you think I could speak to you for a moment about the daily problems you encounter as a slum dweller, such as leaking faucets or lack of hot water or poor disposal of garbage?"

Most of the time no one answered. Sometimes the door opened a crack and an eye or a nose appeared from behind it. Other times a voice would call out, "Ain't no one home."

Boomer asked Deamis if he had been aware that he always referred to people as sir or madam. "That's very important for relating," said Boomer.

Boomer said he would watch Deamis closely and give him advice. He said, "When I think you're relating well enough I'll take you to meet WS." He said that since he had started this job he had related to many people and made many, many friends. He said, "Probably my best friend is Peters. I'd do anything to help him, and he'd do anything to help me." Boomer told Deamis he would take him to meet Peters.

Peters lived in one of the tenements under the El. It smelled. As they entered the building, Boomer began shouting. "Anyone home, anyone home?" Boomer said he was shouting to warn people because there were junkies and winos in the building. "This way we let them know we're coming," he said. "You never want to catch a junkie off guard."

On the stairs they met a woman. She had her head down, and she was swaying as she walked.

As she passed them she said, "Excuse me."

Boomer said, "Oh hello, Mrs. Peters."

Mrs. Peters said, "How-dee-do."

"Oh fine," said Boomer. "I'm just on my way up to see your husband."

Mrs. Peters said, "Who, Mr. Peters?" turned without a word and led Boomer and Deamis up the stairs.

On the second floor, a door to an apartment was open. Boomer whispered to Deamis, "Junkies." He whispered, "That's where Peters spends most of his time."

He said, "Actually, Peters' trouble is he's too generous.

He does anything to help people. He gives away all his money to his friends."

Mrs. Peters opened the door, stepped back and spread out her arm as through she were introducing an act. There on a bed was a man sleeping. He was lying face down. He was wearing a pair of blue overalls and had his shoes and socks on.

Mrs. Peters shook him. "Hey, Peters," she said, "you got company."

"Uh," groaned Peters.

She shook him again.

"Uh," moaned Peters again. He turned over. Deamis saw his face. It was the color of hot chocolate. He had wavy grey hair.

Peters opened his eyes and stared at Boomer and Deamis. He swung his feet over the side of the bed and stood up. He said, "I was in World War II. I was in the South Pacific. I killed thirty, forty Japs."

Mrs. Peters said, "There he goes again. I'm glad you came."

"Don't tell me I didn't kill no Japs," Peters said to Mrs. Peters.

Boomer began talking with Mrs. Peters. Deamis noticed three little children huddled together in a corner. They were staring up at him and Boomer. The El rumbled past the window. It passed so close, Deamis felt he could reach out and touch it.

Boomer said, "Has the welfare worker been here?"

Mrs. Peters shook her head. She looked at Boomer. She said, "I'm not a good woman." Suddenly she began to cry.

"There, there, Mrs. Peters," said Boomer. "There, there." He patted her shoulder.

"It's Ronnie," she said. "It's my son, Ronnie. He's in trouble in school. Why, some boys came over here yesterday and said they were going to kill him if he came back to school. They told me right to my face. He's only ten years old." She started to cry again.

"There, there," said Boomer.

"And you didn't help him none neither," she shrieked at Peters. "You, the boy's father, and you just stood and didn't do nothin'."

"Shut up, woman," shouted Peters. "I give you every cent I have, don't I?"

"No you don't, neither," said Mrs. Peters. "You give everything to your wino friends across the street."

Peters said, "I fought in World War II. I killed thirty, forty Japs."

"Mr. Peters," said Boomer, "that's your whole trouble—you're living in the past—you must live in the present. You must set a good example for Ronnie."

"Don't you worry none about Ronnie," Peters said to Mrs. Peters. "I've got my eye on him."

He said to Deamis, "Why I've got a son over in Brooklyn, he . . ."

"Not by me, you don't," said Mrs. Peters.

Peters said, "He's nineteen years old. He'll protect Ronnie. All I got to do is call him. I just saw him last week. He's a junkie, that boy, he don't care if the sun never shines."

"But what about you, Mr. Peters," said Boomer. "You're the boy's father. You must help him yourself by setting a good example for him."

"What did my father ever do for me?" Peters shouted to Mrs. Peters. "I never did see him after I was five." Then he

119

said, "Sheeit," and stalked out the door. Deamis looked at the children. They were still huddled in the corner as though they were frozen.

"He's going to his wino friends across the street," said Mrs. Peters. She started to cry again.

"There, there," said Boomer, patting her shoulder again. "I'll talk to him." He motioned to Deamis and ran out the door down the stairs after Peters.

Downstairs they saw Peters crossing the street. "There he goes," yelled Boomer.

Across the street, Deamis saw three black, round heads in an alleyway peering out at Peters as he approached them. The black heads had red lips. They looked like a pack of wolves.

"I'll go speak to them," Boomer said.

"Don't," Deamis started to say. But Boomer was already crossing the street.

When Deamis looked up, Boomer was walking back toward him arm in arm with one of the men. He was a large man who needed a shave. Boomer said to Deamis, "This is Clarence. I was thinking there's a possibility we might be able to help him. I was thinking we could take him to the welfare center on the Grand Concourse this afternoon."

"But what about now, man?" said Clarence. "My stomach's hungry now."

Boomer looked at Deamis. He stuck his hand into his pocket and pulled out two quarters. "Here," he said to Clarence. "This is until this afternoon. I'll be back for you then."

When they returned in the afternoon, instead of Clarence they found another large man who needed a shave who

120

said his name was Harris and that he was Clarence's brother. Harris said, "Clarence couldn't come." He handed Boomer a card which said he had a liver ailment and was supposed to report to Morrisania Hospital for treatment once a week.

"Well," said Boomer, "I suppose it won't make any difference." He led Deamis up the hill to the Grand Concourse. Harris loped behind like a large animal.

The Concourse Welfare Center was crowded. Mothers sat in folding chairs holding babies, while secretaries in boots and miniskirts scooted through the aisles.

Boomer whispered to Deamis, "I think it's shameful the way these secretaries dress in front of the poor."

At the head of the room a woman was sitting at a desk in a starched white dress like a nurse. She was writing. Without looking up she said, "What do you want?"

"Help," said Boomer.

"Just fill out a form," said the lady in white without looking up, "and go into the other room."

Another little lady in a white coat stepped up beside them and pointed to Harris and said, "Come with me." Harris stood up. Boomer also stood up. The little lady said to Boomer, "Not you."

The lady led Harris into an office. Boomer followed them. Deamis followed him.

The little lady was saying to Harris, "What is it you want?"

"To get some welfare," said Boomer from the doorway.

The lady spoke to Harris. Name? Address? Is he a veteran? No. Is he married? No. Has he ever been married? Yes. Does he have any children? Yes. How many? One. What? A girl. Name? Lilli. Where is his wife? Brooklyn.

121

Where was he born? Alabama. What was her maiden name? Harris had to think a moment. Culluh. Spell, C-u-l-l-a-h.

What was his mother's name? Father's name? Mother's maiden name? Had he held any previous jobs? Where? How long? Why did he leave? Was he fired? Was he sure? Positive? What was his employer's name?"

Harris had begun to stutter. He kept looking down at the floor and at Boomer and at Deamis. He said he had been a carpenter. He said he had been laid off. He had no money. He had been living with friends. He said he had a liver ailment, and he took the card from his pocket.

The lady took the card. She said, "This says you had an appointment at Morrisania Hospital last week but you didn't keep it, why not?" Harris looked at Deamis. His jaw was trembling.

The lady said, "There's nothing I can do now." She shook her head and told Harris to wait outside. Then she said to Boomer, "The trouble with these people is they simply don't want to help themselves."

Outside, Boomer shook hands with Harris. He said to Deamis, "You see, this is the first step to giving the black man back his dignity."

♟♟♟

Every day at noon Deamis and Boomer walked back to Phurphey's house for lunch. They passed the playground where Rhoda and other women sat on benches and swings with their little children at their feet. They passed un-

shaven men sleeping curled in doorways or standing shivering in front of candy stores. Boomer waved to everyone he passed. To everyone he passed he said, "How ya doin', man."

Every day Deamis and Boomer would see Phurphey talking and laughing with men on the corner of Boston Road or walking very quickly down 169th Street. When Phurphey was walking quickly he would say to Boomer, "Can't stop to talk man, got to run."

Every day Rhoda sent them to Walker's to buy lunch. Walker's was a candy store on the corner of 169th Street and Third Avenue. Walker had a round black face and stood behind the counter cutting meat. When Deamis and Boomer entered, the other customers stopped talking and stared at them.

At Walker's they bought ham, bologna or hot sausages, a loaf of Silvercup bread and a half-gallon of Schaefer beer and Kool-Aid for the children. Rhoda made sandwiches. They sat around the table in the kitchen and ate lunch while the children sat on the floor of the living room and ate in front of the television.

Sometimes James came out of the basement and ate lunch with them. He would nod to Boomer and to Deamis and eat without ever saying a word.

After lunch Boomer went out again to organize. Deamis stayed in the living room and talked to Rhoda and James and Skinny Alice, who visited Rhoda each afternoon. Boomer said to Deamis that he lacked discipline. He said he wasn't sure Deamis would ever be disciplined enough to meet WS. Rhoda said, "You pay him no mind, Deamis darlin'."

In the afternoons, Rhoda, James, Skinny Alice and

Deamis drank Johnny Walker Red or Seagram's or Gordon's and played records. They played "Tell It Like It Is" and "Beauty's Only Skin Deep" and "I Wrote My Baby from Vietnam." Skinny Alice would say, "C'mon, Deamis, dance with me." When they played "Tell It Like It Is," she placed her hands on his shoulders, wiggled her long body into his and swayed from side to side to the music. Deamis smelled her breath and felt her lips, cool and warm on his neck. Sometimes he thought he heard her murmur, "Yeah, Deamis, that's how it is."

Skinny Alice stepped back and said, "Anyway, like I said, Chuckie was real cool—like the first time he took me downtown and bought me a pair of shoes and two new dresses—and he always saw I had my hair done once a week."

"But see what happened with Chuckie was, I didn't know I was supposed to pay him, and he got mad and started beatin' on me wif a coat hanger until finally I gave it to him, you see this mark on my arm? and also he was cool, like there was this girl Charlene who used to work this bar I was workin', and once I stepped on her foot by mistake and I said, 'Excuse me, Charlene' and after that everything I did she called me bitch this and bitch that, so I told Chuckie and he said, 'Next time you just say to her, Charlene why am I a bitch? Why are you angry at me? We're doin' the same damn thing. . . . I didn't mean to step on your foot. So that's what I told her and you know what she said? She said, 'Honey I didn't call you a bitch, I ain't angry at you,' and I didn't have no more trouble with her after that.

"Chuckie's doin' time now, they got him on a armed robbery charge and like I say he's the best old man I ever had even though I didn't know it then, and after Chuckie

there was this man named Cooley (his brother Norville
sings with the Four Tops, you know?) and see you don't
never know about junkies like I don't care what nobody
tells you 'bout it, like with Cooley I didn't even know at
first 'cept he used to beat me a lot for no reason and once
I remember he was sittin' at the bar scratchin' himself and
when I asked him what was the matter with him he said he
was tired, you know how you get? So I didn't catch on
until I found him and some friends just shootin' up—one
of them was shooting some scag right into his neck—and
then he started takin' me to those places where everyone is
shootin' up, you know, they're all with the needles lookin'
for the vein and there's blood all over them and on the
floor and some woman who was supposed to do it in the
bathroom was shootin' it up there right on the floor, and
like I snorted some cocaine, you know in your nose? but
like, I'm not sure of the difference, like when they say
little boys or little girls, you know, like the capsules? I
mean I don't know if little boys is cocaine and little girls is
heroin or what. I think the girls is stronger than the boys,
I'm not sure, but I can tell a woman junkie better than a
man, you know how? By their wrists, if they're swollen up
or not 'bout five times their size, or like you see a girl with
real skinny legs and then you see their wrists and their
ankles and they're swole up? But like I say it's hard to tell
sometimes, like see those marks on my arm, now what that
looks like to you, it looks like dopetracks right? Well it
ain't, see? It's from bein' pregnant.

"That was Obie, see, you know, I was just fifteen and I
was in love and all that, you know, and I was livin' with
my auntie cause my mother died and Obie would always
be comin' round and we'd go over to his pad and he gave
me a key and once I came up there and knocked on the

door and no one answered so I went on in and he was there with two girls and a friend of his and they were high and I was pregnant so I tried to run in front of a car but that didn't do no good and then my auntie was mad, see, because Obie stopped comin' round, cause she wasn't much older than me and I think she kinda liked him too, and one night I took these pills and I got sick and I had my miscarriage right there on the couch in the living room, and they knew I was having it—I was screamin' so loud— but they didn't want to take me to no hospital, and then the next mornin' I passed it out, you know natural-like, and kept it right there in a jar and the doctor told me I had lost my baby and by then I didn't care no more 'bout Obie after I lost my baby, and that's when I met Chuckie, and wished I never saw that mutha-fucka Obie again neither."

Once a week Phurphey played basketball. He played in the evenings in the playground with metal nets where the women sat in the afternoons. The name of Phurphey's team was the Naturals. The Naturals all wore red T-shirts with *Naturals* written on the back in script letters. After they scored a basket the Naturals ran down the court and slapped palms. Deamis stood on the sidelines behind Phurphey's children and watched them running up and down the court slapping palms, and felt as he had when he had watched Susan Stickwell's older brother Mark and his friends playing in Susan Stickwell's driveway.

Once, only five Naturals came to play. One of them got

hurt. He was the big man whose name was Gig. Everyone stood around him as he sat on the ground. Two men helped him off the court between their shoulders.

Phurphey said, "Uh, oh." He walked over to Deamis and said, "Hey, Muldoon, didn't you say you play ball, man?" He said to Gig, "Hey, let my man Muldoon try on your shoes."

Deamis put on Gig's sneakers. He felt the other Naturals watching him as he tied the laces, appraising him like an animal.

He stood up. It was the other team's ball out of bounds. Phurphey said, "You take the big guy." Phurphey was sweating. He said, "Don't play him too close. Give him lots of room.

Deamis met his man at mid-court. He was big, not as tall as Deamis but with thick shoulders. He brushed past Deamis into the middle. They passed it to him and he grabbed it over his head, turned, leaned his shoulder into Deamis and shoved him toward the basket.

Deamis stuck out his arm. The ball bounced free. Phurphey picked it up and threw it to the outside. Deamis broke down the middle. They passed it back to him as he came to the edge of the foul circle. He caught it in the air, took a step to his right past the man nearest him, went up in the air, let the ball slide off his fingertips, watched it arc down toward the basket and heard the clang of the net as it slid through.

The next time they had the ball he went into the middle. They slowed down the play and passed it out into the corners. It went back to him in the center. He faked to his left, stopped, went to his right past his man and up for the shot, felt it leave his hand, felt something smack into his

127

shoulder, saw the ball go through the net as he fell to the ground.

He was up in a second. They had picked off the ball. He was alone in the center. They threw it to him. His man raced over, flung up his hand to block the pass. As he did, Deamis slammed his shoulder into the man's jaw, threw up his shot, saw it spin around the rim and fall through as his man fell to the ground.

Someone slapped palms with him as he ran down the court. He caught a glimpse of Gig standing in his bare feet on the sidelines.

His man came toward him. Someone shouted and the ball floated toward them. The pass was too high. His man leaped for it. Deamis leaped also. He was taller than his man and he flicked it away.

He raced down the center. They were fast-breaking. He felt the wind on his face as he ran. He felt the players beside him becoming still-figures and shadows. He saw Boomer among the crowd on the sidelines. He was standing with Phurphey's little children. They were all watching him play.

They put another man on him. They tried to block up the middle. He went outside and hit a jump shot. He went to the corner and hit another. They put another man on him who floated through the middle, and he found a man open underneath and bounced it in to him.

They tried to move his own man to the outside but he couldn't shoot and Deamis blocked a jump shot, slammed it back at him, and from the sidelines they started applauding.

The other team called time out. Phurphey ran over to Deamis as they stood panting in a circle and said, "Man, why didn't you tell me you could play basketball?"

"You never asked me," said Deamis.

"Sheeit," Phurphey said.

As they were walking home after the game, Deamis heard Boomer saying to Phurphey's little children, "Who wants to play catch in the alley while it's still light out?" Someone said, "The baseball season's over, Boomer." Someone else said, "Why can't you play basketball like Deamis, Boomer?"

As they were walking home Phurphey came up to Deamis. "Hey, Muldoon, I got me a hustle." Phurphey explained that he wanted to bring liquor in from Connecticut and sell it after midnight Saturday nights when the liquor stores were closed. He said, "You get a car Muldoon, we can be partners."

Afterward, Boomer said to Deamis he should be honored Phurphey had asked him to be partners. "It shows you can relate," said Boomer.

"I think he only asked me because he thought I could get a car," said Deamis.

Boomer turned away. "He wish he'd asked me."

The next day Boomer announced he thought Deamis was ready to meet WS. "It's all arranged. He's staying at my pad with my chick till he gets himself together," Boomer said.

Boomer's pad was in the basement of a red-brick tenement on Westchester Avenue. When they entered, a barefoot girl with hair down to her waist leapt out from behind the door at Boomer, flung her arms around his neck, wrapped her legs around his and cried, "Martinez. You've come."

Boomer said to Deamis, "Deamis, I'd like you to meet my chick, Juanita." Juanita said, "Don't you remember me, Deamis? I remember you."

Deamis stared at her. It was Lydia Jane Levy. "Will you stop being so goddamn middle class," Boomer hissed at her. "You know how I feel about that shit. Hey!" he said, "Where's WS?"

Lydia Jane Levy said, "He's in the yard playing with Manuel and the kids." She said, "And guess who's coming later?" She held her nose. "Our friends from Park Avenue." She said, "Pee-you. I know they're supposed to be important but they make me laugh. Just wait until you see them, Deamis."

She and Boomer led Deamis down a dark hallway. It was so dark Deamis almost stepped on someone in a sleeping bag lying on the floor. Lydia Jane Levy whispered to Deamis, "Do you remember my little brother Richard? You boys used to call him some awful names." She added, "Well, that's him."

At the end of the hallway was an open door. There was a cement courtyard and a donkey tied to a chair. A man in a jungle-green camouflage army uniform, combat boots, and a black cowboy hat, was kneeling next to a donkey and jabbering in Spanish to two little Puerto Rican children who sat at his feet. Boomer whispered to Deamis, "That's him." He whispered, "Can't you just *sense* greatness about him."

Boomer walked up to the donkey and said, "Hello, Manuel." He began speaking to the two little Puerto Rican children in Spanish. Deamis didn't know Boomer knew

Spanish. He decided there was a lot about Boomer he didn't know.

Boomer said, "Deamis, this is WS. Wexell Snathely." Without getting up, WS stuck out his hand and said, "Hey there, big boy." WS said he had heard a lot about him from Boomer. "Word travels fast around here," said WS. Deamis wondered what Boomer had told him.

Boomer said to Lydia Jane Levy, "Say, is the pipe ready? I got some good stuff in from the coast." WS said the pipe was in his green bookbag along with his wheat germ, organic honey, and pineapple enzyme tablets. "Protein diet," said WS to Deamis. He winked. "I wouldn't touch any of that pogey bait in these underdeveloped parts of the city. I use only carnation malteds and raw eggs."

WS said, "During the Israeli War for Independence what used to worry me most was the thought of getting stuck in the Sinai without any outlet for my blender." He said, "By the way, you're not Jewish, are you, big boy?"

"Four-thirteenths," said Deamis.

WS whistled. "Big boy," he said, "You sure must be good in arithmetic."

Actually said WS, Israelis were to him a most fascinating people. "Without doubt, the most perplexing aspect of their culture," said WS, "is their insatiable craving for Fanta orange soda.

"Of course," said WS, "the white sands of the Middle East can never equal the rain forests of the Andes or the rice paddies of Nam as a combat zone except for Djibouti or the Crater where I'm thinking of going to next if things prove too tame here." WS said that the best thing about Nam was that whenever he grew depressed he could always go out and jump with the troops. "You know, the VC are all around waiting and you're jumping from the copters and there's all that firing around, and you're yelling, and landing in the middle of them. Whew," he said, wiping his forehead, "a jump like that can keep you going for weeks."

WS said that speaking strictly as a writer he was primarily concerned with answers. "Look, big boy," he said, "did you ever notice how the seagulls drop clams on the rocks to break them open? Well, the answer to that is probably one seagull did it by accident at first and the clam tasted pretty good, so he told his friends about it." WS said the principle was similar to a short story he was writing. "The only trouble is I can't decide whether to call it "The Three Seagulls," or "The Three Clams."

WS asked Deamis if he would like to see his diary. "It's some of my best writing," he said. "I was younger then. I still believed art was accidental and in those goddamn filthy bastard critics. I still believed that to commit yourself to writing professionally involved a divorce from the conventional professions, those same conventional professions that provide the dramatic materials for future creation. It was before I turned bitter and burned my novel, and decided to dedicate my entire life to art. And got this." He lifted up his black cowboy hat. WS had snow-white hair.

"And this." He lifted up his trouser leg. WS had a wooden leg. "Plastic," he said. "I could have had it wooden but they said this was the latest model. It's a PTB. Patella Tendon Bearing. BK. Below the knee."

"I'm sorry," said Deamis.

"Forget it, big boy, forget it," said WS. "Say, I wonder if I could ask you a favor, big boy. I wonder if I could tell you my life story."

"All right," said Deamis.

WS said he was born in Russiaville, Indiana ("In the

fifties, during the McCarthy period, they changed the pronunciation to Rooshaville. Last year the whole town was blown away in a tornado."); received the highest college board scores in the history of the high school ("They refused to believe it was really me."); studied for the priesthood for seven months ("I kept seeing God behind every bush."); spent a year in a Greenwich Village loft writing a novel ("Yeah, the goddamn filthy bastard critics all rejected it.").

WS said, "I used to spend days locked in my room reading—Dundee Corbett and Milo Milt—They were my favorites. Rusty Truax was okay (did you ever read his *Mysticism, Hasidism and the American Indian?*) except for his goddamn use of the pluperfect subjunctive. Those guys really knew where it was at . . . Milto, Dundee and Rusty. Could they write! Could they think!

"The next summer found me driving a cab in Mexico City. That's where I got my first piece of ass. I was twenty then. Yeah, I was a late bloomer. Her old man owned the fleet. We used to do it in the back seat of his '38 Buick.

"Well, after that I couldn't stop. I mean I've been queered in Cairo, blown in Beirut, douched in Damascus and reamed in Rabat. I rode a steamer up the Nile from Wadi Halfa to Khartoum. It's when you see those black women unloading the cargo on their heads in the sunset that you start getting the willies. From there, I took a dhow to the Seychelles where I lived with a native of French blood in a hut by the Indian ocean. First, I had to get her mother's permission. Then I came down with a terrific case of the crabs. Damn near tore a hole in my underwear from scratching so hard."

WS said that speaking as a writer few things gave him as much pleasure as writing a simple declarative sentence.

"It's like hitting a good three iron. They had a terrific course in Saigon, you know, but the VC were always putting their spider holes in the goddamn sand traps."

Lydia Jane Levy sang from inside, "Ready."

"By the way," said WS to Deamis, "I've just written a poem I don't think you've seen." He took a piece of paper from his pocket and handed it to Deamis. Deamis read, "My love glides on invisible wings."

"Well?" said Wexell Snathely.

"Well what?" said Deamis.

"Well, what do you think?"

"About what?" said Deamis.

"About my poem."

"Oh, it's very nice," said Deamis.

"I haven't been able to come up with a second line yet," said WS. "If you think of one, let me know."

"Oh, WS," sang Lydia Jane Levy with her hands on her hips. "Everyone's waiting."

"By the way," said WS, "did I ever tell you the story about the three clams?"

Richard had gotten up and was seated on the floor with Boomer. They were passing a long metal pipe and taking deep puffs, making noises as though they were sniffing. A record player was on. A saxaphone was playing softly.

WS sat down on the floor. "C'mon, big boy," he said to Deamis. "You sit down here next to me."

Richard puffed on the pipe. "Had a good trip last week," he said.

"Me too," said Lydia Jane Levy. "Too bad you weren't with us," she said to Boomer.

"Where did you go?" asked Deamis.

Richard began to cough. He looked at Boomer. "Oh, man," he said.

134

WS said to Deamis, "Big boy, you got a lot to learn."

They passed the pipe to Deamis. WS said, "Suck it in deep and hold it down there."

Boomer said to Deamis, "See, cat, all this stuff they try and tell kids about dope is a lot of shit. Even with smack. Like the only way you can get addicted is when you're on the Jones and you shoot up again before you come down. But see if a kid lives at home with his folks he's got to show up for things like meals, right? So he's got to come down or else his parents will know there's something wrong, right?"

Boomer said that now not even their lies would work because the Revolution had gone too far. "Like now the only thing that ever happens whenever there's a large bust is a lot of kids die of ODs because the dealers are in such a hurry trying to unload they don't cut it all." Boomer said all the lies they were being fed about dope were merely the last gasps of an oppressive society. "It's strictly a class thing," said Boomer. "Our entire class is being oppressed." He added, "You might as well face it Deamis, we're all niggers."

There was a knock at the door. Everyone looked at everyone else. "Jesus Christ," muttered Lydia Jane Levy. "It's them." WS said, "Now don't worry, we don't have to put the stuff away, they won't even know what it is," he said.

He winked at Deamis and walked out of the back door into the courtyard. "It's better if they see him out there with Manuel and the kids," said Boomer. "Good for the image."

Lydia Jane Levy whispered to Deamis, "Wait till you see this. Pee-you."

Boomer went to open the door. Deamis heard a man's

and woman's voices talking animatedly. Someone scurried through the dark hallway past him and out the back door into the yard. It was a man in Bermuda shorts and red sneakers with a camera slung over his shoulder. A woman scurried after him.

Suddenly she stopped. "Why, Deamis," she cried, "what are *you* doing here? Does your father know about this? Deamis, I think it only fair to tell you that Susan is already married.

"Lester," she called to the man who had just scurried past them. "Oh Lester lamb, look who's here."

"What?" called the man.

"Lester lamb, it's Deamis."

"Hello, Mr. Stickwell," said Deamis.

"Er, Deamis," said Mrs. Stickwell, "I think it only fair to tell you Lester has only recently accepted a position with a large philanthropic organization for considerably more remuneration. You know, Deamis, riches are every bit as important as breeding."

Mr. Stickwell said to Deamis, "Want to make some money? Want to make a million bucks? Well, I can do it for you. I've always liked you, Deamis." He said his organization was currently investigating the possibility of investing in local self-help programs with an idea to marketing and franchising in the not too distant future. "They really seem to have something here," he said. "They really have a way with minority types, don't they?" He whispered to Deamis, "Confidentially, I think this WS is a true genius."

Lydia Jane Levy whispered to Boomer, "I can't watch this anymore." Boomer stood up. "C'mon, Deamis," he said, "we've got to get back to our people."

Lydia Jane Levy leapt at Boomer. She flung her arms around his neck and wrapped her legs around his. "Good-bye, Martinez," she whimpered. She hugged Deamis, then held her nose and pointed toward the Stickwells. "See what I mean?"

WS came in and shook hands with Deamis. At the door he said, "The next time you come I'd like to show you my diary. That was some of my best writing. I was younger then. That's how I'd like you to think of me."

As they walked back toward Phurphey's, Deamis said, "Boomer, why do you call Lydia Jane Levy, Juanita? And why does everyone call you Martinez?"

Boomer stopped walking. He turned to Deamis and put his hands on his hips. "My God! Deamis!" He said. "Are you that insensitive? Are you really that insensitive? Didn't it ever occur to you that there are some things in our pasts both Lydia Jane Levy and I would prefer to forget? Couldn't you even understand that?"

Boomer turned away. "WS asked you to see his diary. He never asked me. I wish he'd asked me."

When Deamis returned home, Phurphey said he had something important to speak to him about. "Don't you say nothin' to Boomer, but they're lookin' for Obie." Phurphey said that Obie's problems were that he had too many women. He said one of them had forgotten to write down a number Obie had played off and the number had come in and the collector wouldn't pay him without the slip. "So, like Obie owes this cat four hundred dollars so he's hidin' out. So he's not workin' his block so our bankroll is in trouble."

Phurphey said, "So like maybe you come 'round with me next week." He said, "You done it before, so maybe the white man will change the Kingsnake's luck again."

The next week Deamis received a phone call from his father. "Nigger pussy, eh?" his father said. "They're the best kind." He said, "What do you say I come up there before you leave for school and you line me up with something? Not too dark, and with big tits."

"But they're my friends," said Deamis.

"Don't worry," said his father, "I'll drive my new maroon Imperial with the portable secretary table in the back seat that turns one hundred eighty degrees and has a typewriter and reading light with it. Those people like that kind of thing."

The same week Deamis received a letter. It read:

"Dear Deamis:

I think it only fair to tell you my name did not become Susan Stickwell Thistle but Susan Stickwell Horton. I am married to Norton Horton, Jr. His aunt is related to a Byrd. In Virginia. Norton has two children from two previous marriages, Fern who is eleven and Fawn who is nine. We are expecting one of our very own in the fall named Alexander or Alicia. As the children love animals very much we also have two armadillos named Sam and Sylvie, a borzoi named Justine, a Burmese champagne kitten named Desmond, a mongoose named Gleason, two hamsters named Aurelius and Beauregard and a tyra tree weasel named Bertram. Norton hasn't been to the office for the past two weeks owing to pains in his stomach.

Sincerely yours,

Susan Stickwell (Thistle) Horton.

P.S. I never knew what a tyra tree weasel was until I met Norton."

While Boomer organized in the afternoons, Deamis began going with Phurphey. Phurphey said, "The whole thing is they got to trust you." He said, "If they trust you, you got everything. If they don't trust you, then you ain't got sheeit."

They walked to the playground where the women sat with their small children. Phurphey went up to one of the women. "What number you playin' darlin'?" he said softly in her ear.

"Hey, Kingsnake we been waitin' for you."

"Kingsnake, where you been?"

"I been busy, baby. What you playin' today darlin'?"

He took out a pencil and piece of paper from his pocket. The women gave him money, and he wrote it down. A woman bent down and whispered in his ear and they both laughed. "Ain't got time for that now, girl."

They went up to men sitting on the stoops and standing in front of the stores.

"Hey, Kingsnake, how you doin', man?"

"Hey, nigger, what's happening?"

"Looks like you doin' all right."

"Oh, I'm hangin' on."

Phurphey took out his pencil and paper.

"What you playin', man?"

"What you think, Kingsnake?"

"Anything you want, man."

"Oh I been thinkin' bout the foah."

"Yeah gimme a deuce on the foah."

"Gimme a buck on the three, man."

"You say the three, man?"

"Yeah gimme a buck on the three."

They went into the alley. Phurphey took out the piece of paper from his pocket and counted the money he had collected. He said they were at Saratoga now and that the first race didn't go off till two o'clock. He said, "We got till after three."

Phurphey counted $78. He said, "First lesson, Muldoon, the first number is always the heaviest." He looked down at the piece of paper. It was filled with numbers he had written. He did some more writing on the paper. He said, "Got too much on the four." He said, "Zero, one, two, three we're ok, four . . . those fools bet $34, that's $272. Five, six, we get hurt but not too bad, seven, eight, nine we're home free."

He pointed to a nail on the side of the wall. He put the piece of paper on the nail. "First lesson, Muldoon," he said, "they can't get nothin' on you if you don't have nothin' on you, right?"

They walked out the alley into the street down toward the El. They walked into a bar. Phurphey sat down at the counter. The bartender stared at Deamis. Phurphey said, "He's all right."

"Gimme a Johnny Walker," he said to the bartender. "I got to make a phone call." He looked at Deamis, "Make it two."

Phurphey went to the phone booth. When he came back he said he had bet off some of the four. He looked at his watch. It was ten after three. He said, "Got to wait another ten minutes."

In ten minutes Phurphey made another phone call. Then he walked past Deamis out the door. Deamis rushed after him. Phurphey was walking very quickly. He was looking straight ahead. "I got hurt," he said. "It was the five." He said, "That crazy Obie if he hadn't gotten himself mixed up with that woman and lost his bankroll I wouldn't have had to bet off the four. He said, "First lesson, Muldoon, you gotta have the money."

They were walking past the playground. "Now watch me," Phurphey said. "I got to pay back ninety-eight dollars on the five and I only took in seventy-eight not counting the thirty-four I had to bet off on the four and I had twenty-five myself goin' in so that makes forty-four, sixty-nine so I got to get me twenty-nine. He said, "First lesson, Muldoon, you go to those fools who lost and take their money for the next number to pay off those other fools."

At the playground they approached a woman. Phurphey whispered, "Five, darlin'."

"Five?" cried the woman. "Oh, Lord I knew it was goin' to be the five. I dreamed it last night." She took a dollar out of her pocketbook. "Seven. Now Kingsnake, I'm countin' on you, baby."

They walked up to the other woman. "Five, darlin'," Phurphey whispered to each of them. Sometimes he said, "Sorry, baby." The women each gave him more money. When he had collected enough he went to the women who had won and paid them.

They walked back to the men in front of the candy stores. Phurphey said to Deamis, "Some of these niggers that just come up from the South they bet all the number 'cause they think they gotta win that way. Those dudes, they're so stupid they don't know it only pays eight to one."

As they were walking a car passed them, slowed down, and crawled alongside them. A white man was driving. Phurphey said, "Uh, oh," and walked over to the car, got inside the front seat and sat down next to the driver. As they talked they both stared straight out the front window.

Phurphey got out and walked back to Deamis. He said, "Man, I sure was lucky I was with you, Muldoon. That was the cat Obie owes the four hundred dollars to. I told him you were a cop and I couldn't do nothin' for him now and the dude believed me. Sheeit, Muldoon, you a cop."

He stopped walking and stared at Deamis. "You know, those cats are mean mother-fuckers. They'd stick a knife in your heart sure as sheeit. If you ever see one of them hangin' round, you know you better get on out of there and do it quick." He said, "You just get on the first train you see and you take it. It don't matter where you go but don't let your face be seen for three whole days and three nights."

They walked back into the alley, counted the money, and hung their paper on the nail. There was forty-eight dollars. Phurphey said, "We're OK unless it's the four or the seven and we still won't get hurt too bad." He said, "First lesson, Muldoon, the second number don't come in as hard as the first, the third comes in harder than the second but not as hard as the first."

They walked out of the alley to the street and back down toward the El to the bar. Phurphey went into the phone booth. When he came out he motioned to Deamis and walked quickly out of the bar. Deamis rushed out after him. Phurphey was walking very quickly looking straight ahead. Suddenly he stopped walking, smiled, laughed, and slapped Deamis on the back. "Well, Muldoon," he said, "looks like the white man has changed the Kingsnake's luck."

All that week Deamis went around with Phurphey. He came to know the women in the playground. He came to know the men on the stoops and the corners. He came to know about the number. He learned there was a Brooklyn and a Manhattan number, that the Brooklyn number was the last three figures of the daily racetrack attendance and that they could always check it the next day in the *Daily News*. He learned that the Manhattan number was the digit to the right of the decimal point of the total winnings of the first three races, that the second number was the total of the first five, the third the total of the first seven, and they could always check it the next day in the *Daily News*.

He learned that the number was bet all over the city;

that in places in Harlem people got up at five in the morning, and that before they went to work they bet the number; that they took no bets after twelve when the collector came 'round. In the alley he learned the difference between straights and single action. Under the El he learned how to combinate.

He learned that Phurphey played single action where there was no collector because he didn't have enough money to take straights, but that he could call a collector to bet off a number. He learned that the straights paid six hundred to one, that there were nine hundred ninety-nine possible numbers, and that you gave fifty dollars or sometimes one hundred dollars to the runner for a tip—but that in single action no one ever paid the runner anything at all. "First lesson, Muldoon," said Phurphey, "the little man ain't got sheeit."

In the late afternoon after the third number had come in, Phurphey and Deamis sat on wooden folding chairs with the men outside Walker's. They drank liquor from paper cups or from a bottle wrapped in a brown paper bag and talked about the number. Each afternoon Walker came out and said, "Sheeit, Kingsnake, the way you winnin' these days this boy must be teachin' you your business." And he winked at Deamis.

Every night after dinner, after Boomer had gone out again to organize, Deamis sat in the steamy kitchen and helped Rhoda wash the dishes. Deamis watched her moving her thick rich brown arms as she wiped the dishes with her apron into the soft folds of her body. When she wasn't looking, Deamis would reach his hand into the frying pan on the stove for a piece of leftover meat or chicken. Rhoda would slap his hand, then laugh and shake her head. "Deamis," she would say, "you are worse than my own children."

In the mornings he would find notes she had left for him under his pillow on folded lined paper. They read:

"Beyond all dark clouds there is a silver lining. After the storm the sun will shine through. Take special care of yourself, eat right, get enough sleep and all will be well for you.

"Peace Profound."

Or: "Keep working as you have been. Life can be cruel but now you will see it through.

"Peace Profound. God is Divine."

Or: "We all have our problems, one way or the other. This is a world of troubles. I feel concerned about you and yours. Have faith in God and in yourself and all will be right for you.

"Peace Profound. God is Divine. Love is Happiness."

Rhoda told Deamis not to say anything to Boomer but James was supposed to have gone into the army two months ago but he was afraid. Rhoda said that was why he had been staying in the basement. "You know, in case anyone comes to the house." Deamis nodded. Rhoda said, "He's gettin' himself together."

She said, "Now don't you go sayin' nothin' to that crazy Boomer." She said, "Sometimes I think that boy must be a Communist or somethin'."

Saturday nights they partied. After the Gordon's and Johnny Walker Red was all drunk, after everyone had gone home and the children were asleep in their underwear and the empty bottles and filled ashtrays lay on the floor and Phurphey and Rhoda lay sprawled on the couch in front of the TV asleep in their clothes with their mouths open—

145

Deamis went into the back room to sleep. He half heard Phurphey's faraway snoring, felt Boomer's and James's soft breathing about him, and he began to dream.

Deamis dreamed. Deamis dreamed he saw the Naturals. They were playing basketball out on the playground with the metal nets. The Naturals were wearing their red T-shirts and they were laughing and shouting and slapping palms as they ran up and down on the court. It was evening and the first stars had come out and the crowds stood on the sidelines. In the crowd Deamis saw Phurphey. He heard Phurphey saying, "Sheeit, Muldoon, why didn't you tell me you could play basketball?" Then he felt himself taking off his shoes and putting on his sneakers, and he saw the Naturals had stopped playing and were watching him as he tied his laces.

Deamis dreamed he was stepping out onto the center of the court, and Phurphey was throwing him the ball, and then they were all running down the court, passing the ball to each other, laughing and shouting, and slapping palms. Deamis was dribbling toward the basket. He threw up a jump shot and knew as it left his hand it was going to be good.

Then he was rushing back up court. Arms up like branches, elbows out like swords. Deamis lunged for the ball, stole it away and dribbled back down court. He felt his man just a half step behind him. He felt himself dribbling to the foul line, stopping for a second, then racing again toward the basket. He felt the ball slip off his fingertips and knew again as it left his hand it was going to be good.

He felt himself fighting for rebounds. He felt himself blocking shots, he felt himself pushing off, going to the corners, breaking down the middle. He felt himself always a half step ahead of his man. He felt the wind on his face as he ran, the players behind him becoming still-figures and shadows. On the sidelines he thought he saw Boomer. He was standing under the basket with his thick glasses. He thought he saw Boomer's father. He thought he saw Susan Stickwell and Lydia Jane Levy and Skinny Alice and WS. They were all watching him play.

He dreamed they played on through the night. His shirt was wet and his body was trembling. Yet he couldn't stop dribbling, he couldn't stop running, he couldn't stop jumping. He was at one with the basket. He had *the feeling* that no one could take away from him. He felt it more strongly than he ever had before. He was dribbling faster and faster. He was running harder and harder. He was jumping higher and higher, through the wind and to the stars. . . .

One Friday afternoon, as Deamis and Phurphey sat outside Walker's with Walker and the other men, Phurphey said, "Uh, oh," and walked quickly inside. A car screeched to a halt, a car door slammed and a man rushed up to them. He was white. "Where's the Kingsnake?" the white man hissed.

Deamis started to point inside but the man next to him said very slowly, "Kingsnake? I don't think I know that name."

Another man said, "Kingsnake? Kingsnake? Now let me see. No, ain't heard that name 'round here before."

Walker said, "Kingsnake, hmm," and scratched his round black head. "Kingsnake, hmm, now let me see . . . you know, I think there's some cat 'cross Boston Road answers to that name but there ain't no Kingsnake here."

The white man went away. Deamis turned to the men, who sat staring out across the street. He stared into their blank black faces. And suddenly he longed to be one of them. He longed to be sitting there with them and Phurphey every day in the late afternoon after the third number. He longed to be sitting in the kitchen with Rhoda, clutched by her milk chocolate arms into the fleshy folds of her body. He longed for Walker to say, if someone ever came looking for him when it was time for him to return to Dooton, "Deamis? Now let me see. No, I don't think I know that name. No, ain't no Deamis here."

Phurphey appeared from inside Walker's. "Sheeit, Muldoon, we gotta move," he said. He started walking very quickly toward the El. Deamis jumped up and followed him. "Look," he said, "them cats'll be back. They'll cut your heart out sure as sheeit if they find you. I'll go call Obie and tell him better get that damn money. You get on the first train, see? First lesson, Muldoon, don't show your white ass round here till after sundown tomorrow night."

Deamis raced to the El, and grabbed the downtown train to 149th Street. Crowds of men stood together on the street below him. He ran down the wooden platform into the subway, jumped into a number two train that was sitting in the station and rode it into Manhattan.

At Ninety-sixth Street he changed to a local. He stood in the first car and peered out into the tunnel at the tracks crisscrossing and the lights flashing green and red and orange. They passed an abandoned station he had never

148

seen before. It was dark and the walls were filled with graffiti. He looked across to an express train that was passing them. He saw the passengers in the express. It looked as though the trains were standing still.

At Forty-second Street he raced out the door to the BMT train and rode it downtown to Fourteenth Street. At Fourteenth Street he ran downstairs for the Canarsie train. He stood in the first car and watched it come up out of the ground and run past tenements, large empty lots, apartment projects and gate crossings where there were stones between wooden ties as though they were out in the country.

He took a train to Broadway station, switched to one that sloped through the back side of Queens along the cool green fields of a cemetery, past stocky brick apartments and two-family homes with square, squat lawns. He stayed on the train through the rush hour. He rode the New Lots train out to Brooklyn where it became an El again, then took it back under the ground.

He rode deeper and deeper into the tunnels. He kept looking behind him and changing trains. He stood in the first car and peered out at the twinkling yellow lights. He tried to find lines he had never traveled before, stations whose names he had only imagined. He wondered if he could ride the subway forever, sleeping on empty seats, eating at Sabrett food stands, and riding through the bowels of the earth to the farthest corners of the city.

Late at night he found himself on a strange line, and found himself the only person on the platform. He heard the echo of his shoes as he walked. A train came in on the other side of the station. Through the windows of the cars he saw a couple on the opposite platform. They were facing the tracks and holding hands and moving sideways along the station as though they were dancing.

The train passed on. The couple vanished. Deamis was alone waiting for his train.

Then he heard it. He peered over the edge and saw it deep inside the tunnel. The front of the train was the head. The lights of the train were the eyes. Just as it came into the station it gave two short whistles. Deamis watched it slither in like a snake. But as the first car passed him, Deamis realized there were no passengers on the train. One by one the cars went by, till without stopping the train slunk out again into the tunnel. Long after the train had passed, long after he had caught another and ridden it through the night and the next day, Deamis was certain the train had winked at him.

Phurphey was sitting on the couch, reading the *Daily News* when Deamis returned, Saturday night. "Sheeit, Muldoon," Phurphey said when Deamis entered, "where you been? I been waitin' on you."

"Are you all right?" gulped Deamis. "Is everything all right?"

"Sheeit, Muldoon, the old Kingsnake took care of everything. The man's gone, and we're celebrating. Hey, here's ten bucks, you go out and get us some Johnny Walker Red. We gonna party for three whole days and nights now."

Outside, Deamis saw a purple Imperial convertible parked at the curb. A woman wearing a blond wig was getting out. It was Skinny Alice. As Deamis approached her the car sped off. Deamis caught a glimpse of the driver. He was white.

Skinny Alice said, "You never guess where I been, that man he took me to this real nice place downtown. They served this salad all high like a mountain with this scoop of white cheese and a little red cherry on top. And sheeit, you never guess what was in that car, there was this table in the back seat with a typewriter and a reading light that turned all the way around."

At Phurphey's the record player was on. Phurphey's children were dancing in the living room. They were waving their arms and shaking their skinny little bodies and falling down all over the living room. Phurphey shouted, "That's my kids, they sure can dance."

He said to Deamis, "Hey, you hear about Boomer, Muldoon?"

"No," said Deamis, "what?"

"He was deselected. The man was here today. I told them you could take his place, but you weren't here."

"But why?" said Deamis. "Why did they do that?"

Phurphey shrugged his shoulders. "It's like I been trying to tell you, the little man just ain't got sheeit." He said, "Hey, I'm goin' out to get me some Gordon's. You have some of that Johnny Walker Red and forget 'bout Boomer cause there ain't nothin' you can do."

Deamis felt someone touch his shoulder. It was Skinny Alice.

Skinny Alice pushed her body into Deamis's. She took his hand and led him through the sheet into the bedroom.

151

"Deamis," she whispered. "I'm wet as water. Kiss me, baby. Kiss me hard."

Suddenly the front door slammed. "Oh my God!" shrieked Skinny Alice, "It's Obie! He'll kill me!"

She rushed back into the living room. Deamis followed. But it wasn't Obie. It was Boomer. He was standing in the middle of the living room holding his suitcase. Skinny Alice said, "Have a drink, Boomer."

Boomer didn't move. Deamis noticed his hair was wild and his shirt was out of his pants, and he was panting as though he were out of breath. His glasses looked large as saucers. Deamis realized he had never seen Boomer without his glasses.

"You knew," Boomer shouted. "You've all known. But no one ever told me." He put his head into his hands and sank down onto the floor.

No one spoke. The record player was going:

Deamis took a step toward Boomer. He placed his hand on Boomer's shoulder. "Don't touch me," shrieked Boomer. "Don't touch me, you bastard!"

Deamis drew back in fright. "It's all your fault," Boomer shouted at him. "None of this ever happened before you started coming around. It's been bad luck for me since the first time I met you.

"And Phurphey doesn't like you either. The only reason he's nice to you is because you're good in basketball."

Deamis started. "Just ask Phurphey if you don't believe me," snarled Boomer. "Why don't you go ask him?"

Deamis looked around. Skinny Alice and Rhoda were standing in the corner with their mouths open next to the little children. The record was over, and making a scratching sound.

Deamis stared at Boomer. "It's not true," he said. Then he rushed past Boomer out of the door.

It was a muggy night. Radios were playing and men were sitting outside on stoops and on folding wooden chairs. Deamis raced up to a group of them. "Have you seen Kingsnake?" he gasped, out of breath. "I'm trying to find him."

"Kingsnake?" said one man. "No, he ain't been round here."

There was another group at the corner. Deamis ran over to them. "Have you seen Kingsnake? I'm looking for him."

The men looked up at him. Someone said, "Kingsnake? No he ain't been here tonight."

Deamis ran to Walker's. There were men standing outside talking and laughing. "Have you seen the Kingsnake?" asked Deamis. "I've got to find him."

The men stopped laughing and talking. There was a silence. One man said, "Kingsnake? That's a name I ain't heard round here before."

Another man said, "Kingsnake? Don't think I know no Kingsnake round here."

Deamis raced inside. Walker was standing behind the counter. "Walker," cried Deamis. "Walker, I've got to find Kingsnake. It's very important. The men outside won't tell me where he is."

Walker stared at Deamis. He scratched his round, black face. "Kingsnake," he said, "Kingsnake, now let me see...."

Deamis's stomach dropped. "But don't you know me, Walker? Don't you know me anymore? I see you every day. We sit on the stoop and talk about the number. Please, Walker."

"Kingsnake," Walker said again. "You know I think there's some cat 'cross Boston Road answers to that name, but no there ain't no Kingsnake here."

Deamis felt tears coming to his eyes. Then he fled out of the door.

He started to run. He started running back to Phurphey's house, but as he ran he was suddenly afraid. He was afraid of seeing Phurphey.

He felt himself running toward the playground. There was a group of men on the sidewalk talking. He didn't want them to see him so he ran across the street. A car slowed down. He didn't want the car to see him so he ran into the alley.

Then he felt someone touch him on the shoulder. It was Skinny Alice. He felt her leading him out of the alley back to the street. He heard her saying, "It wasn't your fault, baby. You didn't have nothin' to do with Boomer."

He felt Skinny Alice taking him. Her arms were around him. Her body was close against him. She was saying, "I'm goin' to make it all right, baby. I'm goin' to make it all right."

They walked across the street past little stores and street lamps. Deamis caught a glimpse of the street sign. It said Franklin Avenue.

They turned into a path and walked up to the house. Skinny Alice put her key into the lock and they walked inside. He caught a glimpse of the number on the porch. It said 1369.

Inside it was dark. There was a winding staircase. Skinny Alice stopped and ran her hands along Deamis's body. He felt his blood pulsing. She started to lead him up the stairs.

Suddenly she turned. He felt her body against him. He felt her arms grasping his neck. He felt her lips, cool and

154

warm against his. He tried to escape her lips, but they were pressed firm against his. He tried to escape her grasp but her arms clung to his neck. He tried to escape her body but she stuck her leg between his and pulled him closer to her.

Then he heard a clock. Ding dong, ding dong, it went. Dong ding, dong ding. In the darkness the chimes sent shivers down his spine.

He recognized the name of the street. He remembered the number on the porch. Suddenly he realized he had come home.